HEART STRINGS
By Lynne Waite Chapman

Copyright © 2016 by Lynne Waite Chapman
Published by Take Me Away Books
Cover design by Cynthia Hickey

ISBN-10:1-944203-62-1

ISBN-13:978-1-944203-62-7

To Jeanette

Blessings

Lynne Waite Chapman

Chapter One

How about this for a depressing thought? I'm forty-three, and all my worldly possessions fit inside a rented Cargo Van. I promise I'm not a deadbeat. I'm not a drug addict or alcoholic, but I'd come close to being homeless.

I've been on the road for eleven hundred miles—the last two hundred on this crummy secondary road, under cloudy skies and drizzle. Gotta love the Midwest. Destination: Evelynton, Indiana, my hometown, where I'd be willing to bet the neighborhoods hadn't changed in twenty-five years. Same houses, same intolerable, narrow streets. The same five thousand residents who mowed lawns on Saturday morning, went to church every Sunday, and never locked their doors. The continuous circuit of uneventful small town life. Little did I know I wouldn't get through the summer before I'd be longing for such monotony.

I hadn't driven more than a few blocks into town, when a runner barreled off the curb and splashed into the street. My foot jerked to the brake. I leaned my full weight on the pedal and punched the horn.

His eyes remained focused straight ahead, never even glancing in my direction. The tires squealed as the van lurched to a halt, and I braced for the avalanche of boxes and suitcases that would come tumbling toward the front seat. The runner never broke stride, seemingly ignorant of his brush with death. I slammed the gear shift into park and pounded on the horn again. It released some anger, but still didn't get his attention.

"Are you deaf as well as blind?" My words echoed inside the van.

He continued running. Obviously an experienced runner, the man's lean muscles held not an ounce of fat.

Idiot.

I silently cursed him and pushed boxes to the back. I picked up a paper cup now lying on the floor, and threw a couple napkins at the puddle of cold coffee. After a few deep breaths, I put the van into drive.

Thank goodness for good brakes. How had that man escaped being hit? I wondered if I'd almost made some woman a widow. The mere word brought back ugly memories.

My life ended the day that phone call came for me. It knocked the life out of me. The message was clear. I was alone—first time ever. My husband Marc, encourager, protector, was gone. It took a while to face the reality of life alone and the shock. I'd always imagined I'd played a part in supporting us—that I had a real writing career. It didn't take long to understand the few magazine articles I sold did little to pay for the condo, the car, the life.

Now, five years later, I had nothing. How had I spent all this time in limbo? How many meaningless, low paying jobs, living from paycheck to paycheck? It was like standing on the beach I loved so much, blissfully staring at the ocean while waves slowly stripped sand from under my feet. I sank deeper and deeper, to my knees, my chest. About the time the waves threatened to wash over me—no more savings and not much left to sell—I gave up and cried out to the God I never spoke to. I guess I should have done that sooner, because the strangest thing happened. I was rescued, if you can call it that.

My rescuer wasn't the hero I'd have written into my great novel, just a little old lady—rather, the administrator of her will. A letter, addressed to me, Lauren Grace James Halloren, pulled me back to the hometown I'd never intended to visit again. I was back, for the sake of a paid-for house, and a thirty-five year old car with only ninety-four thousand miles on it. Bless Aunt Ruth, my father's older sister. She remembered me, her last relative.

Sun broke through the clouds and I guided the van onto tree-lined Stoneybridge Drive. As I recalled, Aunt Ruth's house, number 410, would be about half way down the block. My stomach fluttered. Was I nervous?

Maybe just hunger. It had been a long time since lunch.

I scanned house numbers, searching for familiar landmarks, when a bright spot grabbed my attention. Mr. Tall Dark and Handsome stepped out of number 404 and trotted toward a black SUV. This couldn't be an Evelynton resident. His brown slacks and crisp white shirt set off a healthy tan. Big city, all the way. He reached up to brush the raindrops from his hair, and his gaze met mine. I sort of fell into his dark eyes.

Lauren! Let's not get sidetracked now.

I had to shake my head to clear my mind and return my attention to the street in front of me. Too many hours on the road.

The next house was mine—or soon would be— and I pulled into the driveway, parking close to the house. In my side mirror, I watched the SUV pull away from the curb and drive off.

The tidy Cape Cod sat in front of me. A pot of petunias bloomed on the porch, and a massive maple tree hovered protectively over a trimmed lawn. I released the scowl I'd held for the last hundred miles and let my shoulders relax. I really needed neat and tidy.

And there was my new car, as Aunt Ruth's lawyer had promised. A 1975 Chrysler New Yorker station wagon. I eased out of the van, reached my hands toward the sky and stretched to ease tight muscles. Then, I could only study the station wagon. Unbelievable. Could I actually drive this thing? Avocado green, with wood toned paneling down the

4

side, not something I'd have chosen. It wasn't like any car I'd ever even seen. On the bright side, no rust spots, and I'd been assured it ran. Who was I to be particular?

I circled the car and felt the pull to glance to the left of the drive. A dark, weathered blue, two-story sat a mere ten feet away, and a small face peered at me from an upstairs window. The woman seemed pale, with thin colorless hair, but that could've been the effect of the last rays of the late afternoon sun reflecting on the glass. Visible for only a few seconds before she pulled away, she didn't smile or acknowledge me. I wondered if she still watched from the depths of the room.

My gaze slid to the windows below, my heart giving a hard thump at the sight of the man I guessed to be the woman's husband. Big, with shaggy, gray hair, and a five o'clock shadow. He stood his ground when our eyes met. A smile and wave produced no response from him. I blinked first and returned my attention to matters at hand. I was suddenly anxious to be inside.

Three concrete steps led to the small open porch of my new house and the mailbox holding the key. Also, a square, beige envelope that I opened immediately, thinking this was information I'd need before entering.

There wasn't a name on the envelope. Inside was an invitation to the Evelynton high school class reunion. Twenty-five years?

No way. Must be for someone else.

Okay, I knew it was for me but I had no intention of attending. Nobody there I wanted to see. I hadn't even talked to them in a quarter century.

The heavy wood front door swung open revealing a short entry and the living room. The scent of waxed hardwood floors summoned memories, the sounds of giggles and tapping of feet as my toddler legs ran through the room, circling that armchair where a little white haired lady sat.

White haired Aunt Ruth. Had she always been old?

Through an arched doorway to the right, an oval, walnut table remained in the formal dining room. This wasn't my favorite room. There had been meals served on beautiful dishes, I was warned not to break. A corner cabinet housed a few of the precious plates Aunt Ruth treasured. I guessed the full collection hadn't survived, although a few intriguing antique bowls and vases were nestled beside the plates. I didn't remember those

Polka dot sheer curtains hung in the next room— the kitchen. The bright yellow walls I remembered had been painted a softer off-white. I pulled open cupboard doors revealing plain dishes, glasses, and canned goods.

A door off the kitchen led to a roomy screened-in porch, where Aunt Ruth used to sit and read—a cup of tea next to her, on a fragile table. The room sat empty except for a few wicker chairs and a wooden plaque. Hand printed lettering read, "You will live in joy and peace. The mountains and hills will burst into song, and the trees of the field will clap their hands!"

My aunt was a strange lady.

I retraced my steps and inspected a single bedroom and bath before taking the stairs to two very small rooms and another bath. By the time I reached the top of the staircase, I was gasping and pulled open windows to release the stale air.

I'd spent the night in one of these rooms, once or twice, when I was very young. The last time I ventured down the stairs, I'd stretched to set my foot on each wooden step, then tiptoed to peek into the kitchen. Aunt Ruth stirred eggs in a big frying pan. I hated scrambled eggs. Still do.

Personal items—clothes, toothbrush, combs, and soaps—had been removed from the house, but plenty of furniture remained. Carved walnut chairs surrounded the dining table. Above it hung a framed print of people dancing. That was a laugh. When did Aunt Ruth ever dance? This was all evidence of a sweet little old lady, not the stern woman I knew her to be.

So, this is home now.

Wait, not my home, a house.

I planned to stay only to finish paying off debt, and to move on as soon as possible. If a reputable antique dealer could be found, my time here might be shorter than anticipated.

Back outside, I slid open the side door of the van, and leaned in to tug at a couple of suitcases wedged against the seat. After considerable groaning and straining, I freed one and coaxed it to the door. Goosebumps tickled the back of my neck. I peeked at the blue house, and seeing no one, released the breath

I held. Gripping the suitcase, I turned from the van and came face to face with a tall, white-haired man. An involuntary shriek erupted from somewhere deep in my throat, and I latched onto the side of the van to keep from falling in, dropping my bag.

The man stooped to pick up the suitcase, and when he raised up, a smile stretched across his face, and tiny lines crinkled around his eyes. "Sorry. I forget myself sometimes. Should've made some noise." He tipped his head toward the house where the black SUV had been parked earlier, "I'm your neighbor, Wallace Binion." He spoke softly, as if afraid I might scream again. His voice sounded like tires on gravel. "I thought I'd help you unload before the rain starts again."

"Lauren Halloren." I gave him my best smile and shook his hand. "Thank you, Mr. Binion, but I don't want to bother you."

"Call me Wallace. It's no trouble at all. That's what neighbors are for. Miss Ruth James was a nice lady. Always kind to me." He reached past me, picked up one of the larger boxes, and headed to the house with it and my suitcase.

That's what neighbors are for? I'd barely known my neighbors in Tampa.

"Thank you. I appreciate your help. I've been driving for the last two days and...." I was babbling, and Wallace Binion already stood on the front porch, so I pulled out a box and followed.

A man of few words, he made quick work of emptying the van, stacking everything in the living room. At the door, he said, "I'll leave you to get settled. If you need anything, let me know."

"Thank you, Mr. Binion,"

"Call me Wallace."

He made his way across the yard climbed the steps to his house. At least he wasn't one of those people who overstay their welcome.

I locked the van and trudged up the steps one last time. The sun peeked from under gathering clouds, its final beams streaming across the street. The door shut with a satisfying thud. I gathered enough strength to deposit my clothes in the closet and make up the bed in the downstairs bedroom.

Windows closed, curtains drawn, and doors bolted, I let myself feel comfortable. After a shower, I crawled into bed with a book determined to put the last two days and five years behind me.

As I drifted off, a police siren in the distance, sounding out of place in this small town, reminded me how far I'd come.

And how far I had to go.

Chapter Two

A single beam of sunlight shot through the narrow opening in the curtains, blinding me as I awoke. The book rested on my chest, and the bedside lamp still burned.

Disoriented and confused, I turned to my side, away from the sun. My eyes refocused on old-lady, flowered wallpaper. Oh yes, Aunt Ruth's.

Yearning for caffeine overruled the temptation to pull covers over my head. I slid my feet to the cold floor and stumbled into the kitchen to search the cupboards. To my great relief, a half-empty can of coffee sat tucked between the sugar canister and a bag of flour. After loading the coffee maker, I leaned on the counter and waited for the scent of fresh brew. The kitchen contained all the necessities—stove, refrigerator, microwave, but no dishwasher. Aunt Ruth would never have trusted her dishes to that modern convenience.

Gleaming white cabinets accented the soft gray

counter top. Purple lettering, on the wall above the window, caught my eye. "His Mercies Are New Each Morning." Very pleasant. Someone must have redecorated after Ruth died. Funny, it didn't smell of fresh paint.

Cradling the mug, I considered returning to bed, and might have, if a knocking at the door hadn't interrupted me.

Please, don't let it be the neighbor.

I opened the door a crack and peeked out to see a big man cradling a toolbox under one arm. His blue work shirt strained at its buttons across his considerable stomach.

When he caught sight of me, he leaned in and peered back at me through the opening. "Good morning, Ma'am. My name's Ted. You called for telephone installation and Internet access?"

Ugh.

I'd made the appointment before leaving Tampa.

"I sure did." Taking a step back, I let the door swing open. "Come in."

Ted lumbered in and scanned the baseboards while I pointed to my chosen hook-up spots.

"This will be a piece of cake." He smiled. "I've worked here before."

"Uh huh. Great. You go ahead. I'll be right back."

I slipped into the bedroom to dress and run a comb through my hair.

When I returned, Ted was sitting on the floor inserting the final screw into the wall outlet. He nodded in my direction. "Beautiful morning out there."

"Uh huh." I walked to the kitchen for more coffee. Not sparkling conversation, I know, but I've never been fond of small talk, especially in the early morning. By the time I'd filled my cup, Ted was still on the floor, but packing up his tools, so I prepared to let him out.

Instead of getting up, Ted rested an elbow on one knee. "I bet you're Miss James' niece. I heard she left her house to you."

I backed up a step and leaned on the door frame, hoping to discourage further chit-chat. "Yes."

Ted seemed very comfortable on the floor. "Ruth and I went to the same church." He tipped his head back and stared at a spot above my head. "Let me think. She said you were her only family after her brother died. She called you Lauren Grace. Right?"

I was surprised she'd ever talked about me. "I go by Lauren, now. Is there anything I have to sign or are we all set?"

"Ruth was a nice lady, but I don't have to tell you that. She visited the old people and delivered meals when anyone was sick. I can see she kept this house in fine shape, too. I'm glad it went to family instead of being sold to strangers."

I forced a smile. "Thank you. I didn't know Aunt Ruth all that well. It's been quite a few years since I've been in Evelynton. So, is everything set with the phone and Internet?"

"Yep." He finally snapped the lid closed on his toolbox and pushed himself up off the floor.

"Good to meet you." The big man shook my hand and plodded out.

I guzzled my coffee and shut the door as soon as he stepped off the porch.

The day had begun. No chance of going back to bed. I picked up my new phone and dialed the rental company for a van retrieval.

At least one thing had a chance of leaving this town sooner rather than later.

~

While I was cleaning the final evidence of my cross-country trip from the van, a shiny red sedan pulled to the curb. The young man, who popped out of the passenger side, had a ponytail longer than mine. He took his time sauntering up the drive.

"Long Distance Truck Rental, Ma'am. Here for a pick-up."

Ma'am again?

"Great. It's ready to go." I accepted the clipboard and pen, and signed by the X.

Meanwhile, he moved closer to the Chrysler, and stooped to look in the windows. "Um, nice car. This yours?"

I straightened my shoulders and lifted my chin as I handed back the clipboard and keys. "Yes. It's a classic."

"Nice." He slid into the driver's seat of the van and turned the key. A quick wave, an unnecessary revving of the engine, and he squealed tires out of my driveway. The red sedan followed close behind like a baby elephant following its momma.

They were in a hurry to get out of town, too.

My rumbling stomach reminded me this was as

good a time as any to find a grocery store. Car keys in hand, I approached the station wagon with some trepidation. This would be a bit of a comedown from the slick sports car I used to drive. Or even the rented van I'd arrived in.

The heavy door of the old Chrysler swung open with only slight creaking, and the simple act of sliding behind the wheel brought on a desire to sing the Brady Bunch theme song. But the light green vinyl seats were in perfect condition—not a crack or tear. To my surprise, the engine roared to life at the first turn of the key, and the door clicked shut with a solid thunk. I could hear Aunt Ruth's mantra: "You don't have to slam the door. It's a Chrysler."

I found reverse and slowly eased out of the drive. It took all my strength to crank the wheel enough to make a tight turn onto the street. No power steering. How did Aunt Ruth handle this boat?

I hadn't traveled more than a block when my cell phone rang. I fumbled in my bag to find it. Were there laws in Indiana against cell phone use while driving? "Lauren Halloren."

"Ms. Halloren, this is Earl Clooney with Justice Insurance. I'm calling at the request of Smith Williams."

"Can I call you b—"

The man didn't take a breath. "As you know, he was Ruth James's attorney and handled her estate. I've been asked to give you a reminder call about the insurance on the house and the car."

"Insurance? I haven't even thought about it."

Crap. One more thing to add to my list.

As if reading my mind, Mr. Clooney chirped, "No worries, I'll take care of everything. That is, providing you want to remain with the same company. Of course you're welcome to use any you choose. Maybe you have an insurance agent you prefer?"

I shook my head. "No, I don't. I haven't owned a house for a while, or a car. This has all happened so quickly."

Clooney lowered his voice, taking on a tone that reminded me of a funeral director. "I see. In that case, are you aware that at this time you are uninsured? Ms. James's insurance coverage ended upon her death."

Uninsured? I took my foot off the accelerator, turned the wheel, and directed the wagon to the curb.

Mr. Clooney continued in a lighter vein. "I carried Ms. James's insurance for many years and have all the information on the house as well as the car. It would be my honor to take care of your insurance needs, as well."

I let my forehead drop to the steering wheel and scrunched my eyes closed. "That sounds like the best option. When can I come in?"

"I have time right now if you're available. We'll get it taken care of today."

"Oh, thank goodness. Yes, I'm available." After recording his address, I checked the rear-view mirror, pulled away from the curb, and drove five miles an hour under the speed limit all the way to Justice Insurance

Mr. Clooney opened the front door of the one-story office building when I got out of my car. He stood with his feet apart, and hands thrust into the pockets of his ill-fitting, brown suit. "Beautiful day, isn't it? Come on in. I'll show you the way."

I followed him down a long, dimly lit hallway to an office at the back of the building. The center of the room was occupied by a vintage wooden desk surrounded by three leather upholstered chairs. Tall file cabinets lined the wall on one side, and the opposite wall was taken up with a printer, paper shredder, and book shelves.

I took a seat across the desk from him as he began an obviously well-rehearsed spiel. "Welcome to the Justice Insurance family, Ms. Halloren. Rest assured we're ready and able to handle all your insurance needs. Complete home and auto protection, under one roof." He took a breath and flashed a satisfied smile. "As I said, I handled your aunt's insurance needs for many years. Let me begin by saying I'm heartbroken for your loss. Ms. James was a lovely lady."

"Thank you, Mr. Clooney. That's very kind of you."

His chair rocked as he leaned into it. "How about something to drink? Can I get you anything?"

"Yes. Thank you. I would love a cup of coffee."

His cheeks sagged. "Gosh, I'm sorry. I don't have coffee. I stopped drinking it all together. I guess I should've told you before you got your hopes up. That caffeine will kill you." He leaned forward and pointed at me. "Did you know it's a drug? Very addictive." He shook his head, then swung his hand to a compact refrigerator at the side of his desk. "How about some ice cold spring water or fruit juice? Orange? Grape?"

"You know, I'm fine, really. Maybe we should just get to the insurance papers." I massaged my temples to ease tension threatening to blossom into a full-blown headache.

"Certainly." Earl pulled a stack of paperwork from a drawer and slid the top sheet toward me. "I took the liberty of preparing these in advance. All you have to do is fill in your personal information here." He tapped the paper. "Sign where I've indicated on the other pages, and we'll be good to go."

He tented his fingers and looked on while I signed my life away.

~

Fifteen minutes later, I drove my fully insured classic station wagon to Quick Mart Gas and Groceries. Not much of a food selection, but I picked out enough for a few days. I pulled down the tailgate and tucked the two bags of provisions in the back while marveling at the size of the vehicle. Large enough to haul a month's worth of groceries, four kids and a dog, with room to spare.

Back at Stoneybridge, between trips to various cupboards and the refrigerator, I watched my neighbor through the kitchen window. Mr. Binion pulled weeds from around an assortment of what appeared to be vegetable plants. Never would have pegged him as a gardener.

I assembled a sandwich, and sat down to peruse *The Evelynton News*—a quick read. The headline, *Crime Spree Continues, Police Baffled*, took up a third of the first page. A paragraph below told of a theft on Maumee Street, the previous evening. A valuable coin collection stolen. The owner was out bowling and returned to find the back door open—big surprise, it hadn't been locked—and no treasured coins. Apparently, this was the fourth in a string of break-ins over the past three weeks.

I took a bite of sandwich. *Should it be called a break-in when the door was unlocked?*

The rest of the news consisted of weddings, funerals, anniversary parties, and Miss Elizabeth DuPree, of the Beaver Creek Nursing Home, turning one hundred years young on Saturday.

I threw the newspaper into the recycle bin and set about unpacking. My minuscule television fit on an end table in the living room and I positioned the computer and printer to face it. Aunt Ruth would have had a fit over the arrangement. She may have served tea and cookies to her friends in this room, but I had no plans for entertaining. I tore into the boxes, put my last four unchipped coffee mugs and teapot in a cabinet, and placed Marc's favorite mug on the windowsill above the sink.

I unpacked a box of sweaters and pulled open the bottom drawer of the dresser, intending to drop them in, when I paused. A square of paper lay in the bottom of the drawer. No, an old snapshot. I placed the sweaters on the bed and lifted the photo. My heart beat thumped in my ears as I held the picture. What kind of mean trick is this? Marc and I smiled into the lens—our wedding day. How did Aunt Ruth get it?

She'd barely approved of me during my preteen years and hadn't been concerned at all after I left for college. As a single dad, my father hadn't known what to do with me and was visibly relieved to send me off. Then, I met Marc, my perfect match. He had no family either, so we eloped. In this picture, we were on our way to an exciting new life. I'd mailed my father pictures, at his request, with an apology for being disrespectful.

I blew out a long breath and willed my pounding heart to slow. Dad must have given Aunt Ruth the photo—only to have her discard it here. My beloved husband was the only person who had truly loved me, and he was gone. That dark, lonely reality hit hard. I wiped the tears and walked to the kitchen to prop the photo beside his special cup.

To complete a cruel joke, the three remaining boxes were labeled in permanent marker, "Marc." I'd wallowed in my grief for a full year before clearing out his closets. Everything I could stand to part with, I gave away, and packed what I couldn't. Since that day, these boxes, the last of his possessions, remained sealed. I shoved them to the far back corner of a dusty closet under the staircase. Someday I'll be strong enough to throw them away.

A rapping on the door broke my train of thought.

Ugh. I don't have any more appointments.

Leave me alone.

Another knock. Pushing up from the floor, I stared at the offending door, willing the pounding to stop. After another insistent knock, I stalked to the door and flung it open.

Chapter Three

Fully prepared to decline whatever this unwelcome visitor was selling, I stood staring at a woman's back. About my height and size, plus fifteen pounds, blond hair curled at her neck.

"I'm sorry, but I'm really busy."

She turned. The wide grin, the blue eyes, pinged a memory. "Lauren, it really is you. They said your aunt Ruth left the house to a relative. I couldn't think who else it might be."

She paused, allowing me an opening to speak, but nothing came. "You look great. I hope I didn't catch you at a bad time, but I was in town and just had to come over and bring you a housewarming gift." She held up a colorful ceramic pot filled with red and yellow flowers.

She could probably see question marks in my eyes as I held out my hands to accept the gift. "Thank you. That's nice of you." Think, Lauren, a name….

Anita! My friend in high school.

Got it. "Anita, it's good to see you." To my surprise, this was true. I hadn't wanted company, but this intrusion was welcome. "You caught me off guard, and my mind went blank. Umm. Come in."

Anita intercepted my attempt to step aside, enfolding me in a warm hug.

When was the last time I'd been hugged? Tears sprang to my eyes.

Quit it Lauren. Crying? How silly is that?

A few awkward seconds later, she released me and stepped into the living room. "Oh, isn't this nice? It's so cozy."

She plopped down on the sofa with a sigh, and reproduced her famous grin. "It is good to see you, Lauren. My goodness, how long has it been?" Anita waved her hand above her head. "Wait, I know exactly how long. Twenty-five years. I know this because our class reunion is next week. Can you believe it? And you haven't changed a bit. I can't wait to hear all about your last quarter century." The room rang with her laughter.

Anita had changed. The picture of a forty-three-year-old, small-town housewife and mother, she'd developed deeper dimples and lots of smile lines.

"You look great, Anita."

The glad tidings began to fade as I thought of the last twenty-five years. So to avoid regurgitating my life events, I blurted, "Anita, tell me about yourself. What have you been doing?"

"You know I went to business college after high school. Long-story-short, I met my husband, Jake—the love of my life—at my first job. We live in the old Tuburgen estate at the edge of town. Well, it didn't take long for me to become pregnant—twins—and I quit work. Sue and Janey attend college in Chicago."

Kids?

Quite a conversation-stopper for me, I groped for a reply. "Wow. That's great. Twin girls. That must have been fun. How about something to drink? Do you want a can of pop or coffee?"

"Oh, coffee would be wonderful." Anita followed me into the kitchen and rested against the counter while I fiddled with the coffee maker. "Now tell me about what you did. I know you got married after college. Eloped, if I remember right. We all thought that was so romantic. Any children?"

"No." My hand trembled as I pushed the power button. I took a deep breath and stared out the window. "We never had time—then Marc was killed—murdered five years ago."

Anita sucked in a breath and became quiet. I looked at her. Even the pink had fled her cheeks. Her voice came in a hush. "I'm so sorry. I heard your husband died, but.... I can't imagine what it was like. How insensitive of me. I am so sorry I brought up such a painful memory."

"It's okay, Anita. I haven't voiced the words in a long time. Guess I think if I don't talk about it, it will go away."

We were silent for a few seconds.

"New subject. This is a great home." Anita pivoted, scanning the cupboards. "The kitchen is sweet, it doesn't need a thing. Tell me about your plans for rest of the house."

I took deep, calming breaths and handed Anita her filled coffee cup. Then I led the way back into the living room, and wondered how to explain my plans involved selling everything and leaving as soon as possible.

Anita could never tolerate silence. "Do you remember Clair? We're on the reunion planning committee. Wait, who am I kidding? We are the committee—the only ones who do any planning, anyway. You're home just in time. The reunion is next week."

"Did you get the invitation? I left it in the mailbox, just in case."

"Yes, I did. I'm not sure where I put it." I glanced around trying to remember if I laid it down or threw it away.

"Don't worry, I have more. It's two days of fun—a cocktail party Friday and a dinner on Saturday. Isn't that elegant? And you'll get to see everyone."

Ugh. Not my cup of tea.

"I don't know. Crowds are not my thing. Who would I know besides you?"

"Nonsense, you'll know loads of people."

"It's been twenty-five years. What would we have to talk about?"

"You'll be surprised. Wait 'til you see Clair. Remember how she always got us into trouble?"

That made me laugh, and at the sound of Anita's giggle, old memories came rushing into my mind. I missed visiting with friends.

Our laughter stopped short when we heard a blast. The floor vibrated, and the windows rattled. My cup hit the floor, and Anita's spilled in her lap.

Her eyes grew wide. "What was that?"

"It sounded like a gunshot—a really loud gunshot." I sprang to my feet and ran to the door. Anita followed close behind, hissing in my ear, "Don't open it."

That was wise counsel. Not sure why I ignored it. But I grasped the handle, pulled it open two inches, and strained my eyes to scan the surrounding area. Anita laid a hand on my shoulder and stretched to peer over my head. I held my breath.

All was quiet, except for leaves rustling in the breeze. Across the street, faces pressed against window panes. A woman ventured out onto the sidewalk, then a man emerged from the house next to hers and yelled from his porch. "What on earth was that?" The woman shrugged.

With activity returning to Stonybridge, I felt emboldened to step onto the porch as well. Anita inched forward and clung to my arm.

She took a deep breath and laughed. "A truck must have backfired, but it scared me to death."

"Kind of loud for a backfire. But everything seems okay. Let's go back in. I'll pour more coffee."

The distant whine of a siren caused me to freeze with my hand on the door knob.

The noise increased to an ear piercing scream, then silenced, as two police cars skidded to a halt at the curb. The driver of one jumped out and ran to the door of the blue house. The second drew his gun and jogged to the back yard.

Anita pushed me inside and slammed the door behind us. She stood with her back to the door, staring at me with big round eyes.

I pointed her to the window. "Wait here and watch. I'm going to the back room to see what's going on in the yard."

After a few minutes, Anita called from the living room. "Do you see anything?"

I yelled. "The police officer searched the bushes and went to the alley, but he's coming back now." He holstered his gun and entered the back door of the blue house.

"There isn't anything going on up here," Anita complained.

I joined her in the living room. "You didn't miss much back there. He's inside now. I don't think he found anything."

"You were right, not a backfire. Maybe a gun shot? Or an explosion? You know, like a gas grill. I'm trying to remember who lives there. The Wilsons? No, they're on Elm. The Brubakers are on the other side of the street." Anita droned on. Her constant chatter filling the minutes as we maintained vigil.

Before long, an officer exited the house, climbed into his squad car, and sped away.

While Anita stood watch, I knelt to retrieve the spilled coffee cups.

She bounced up and down on her toes. "Someone's coming out."

I glanced up to see Anita bolt outside and down

the steps shouting, "I know him."

By the time I pulled myself up and made it to the porch, she'd corralled the second, younger police officer at his squad car.

I took a seat on the step and marveled at Anita's energy. After many gestures, flapping of hands, and undecipherable words, she stilled and appeared to listen to the man. He punctuated his report with a shrug and got into his car.

As he motored away, Anita returned to sit beside me on the step. "That was Jimmy Farlow. I used to babysit him."

"So, what happened?"

"Clive Barron, that's the guy who lives there, came home to find a prowler in his house. They ran out the back when they heard him. Clive grabbed his 12 gauge and shot from the back door. That's the explosion we heard. He missed, thank goodness. Would you believe he keeps a loaded shotgun in the house?"

"I've only seen him once, but I believe it. He scares me. Did he identify the intruder?"

"No. All he saw was someone in a dark hooded sweatshirt. The guy was long gone by the time the police arrived."

Anita shuddered and hugged herself. "This is terrifying. I have Jake, and our dogs wouldn't let a stranger in the house. But you're alone. How are the locks on your doors?"

"They're good. I checked them out yesterday. Having lived in the city, I appreciate good locks. Besides, what's to steal? An out-of-date computer and an ancient TV?"

Anita chewed on a fingernail. "Maybe since they got shot at today, they'll stop. At any rate, I'll be praying for your protection."

The squeak of a door caused our heads to swivel toward the blue house. A red-faced Clive Barron stood and glared at us for an instant before turning to lock his door. I heard a distinct growl as he stalked to his car.

Keeping her eyes on Clive, Anita leaned toward me to whisper. "Let's go in."

"Yep." We scrambled inside.

"Creepy. Evelynton was always predictable, if not completely soporific, but at least I felt safe. Where'd the crazies come from?"

Anita gathered our cups from the chair where I'd left them, and carried them to the kitchen. "They'll catch those thieves soon, and everything will settle down. Evelynton will be back to the lovely little town it's always been. Let's have that coffee."

Anita retrieved her handbag and smiled. "So, what were we talking about? Oh yes, school. The reunion. You did get the invitation I left?"

I scanned the room again and retrieved the beige envelope from the side table where I'd dropped it the day before. "I got it but didn't know it was for me. As you know, I've lost touch."

"Well, now that you're holding a personalized request, please say you'll come."

I sank into my chair. "You recovered quickly from the shotgun blast."

Anita grinned. "I'm sure everything will be fine. We've never had trouble before, and our police force is on it. What do you say about the reunion?"

"Okay, okay. I'll try to drop in for a little while. But I don't know what I'll wear, and my hair's a wreck." To emphasize my point, I shook hair out of my eyes, confident the action would make it worse and prove my point. "I need a haircut."

"Not a problem. I know the best hairdresser. You'll love her." Anita grabbed the invitation from me and wrote on the back of the envelope.

"I can't wait. You'll have so much fun at the reunion."

I narrowed my eyes. "I said maybe, Anita." I might have emphasized the word maybe more than necessary.

"Un-huh." With a twinkle in her eye, and a lopsided smile, she slapped the invitation into my hand.

Anita's gaze darted to the mantle clock. "Look at the time. This is my day at the charity shop. Boy, will I have a story to tell today." She gave me a quick hug and turned to leave. "Talk to you soon."

I watched her drive away before closing and locking the door.

After proudly placing the flowers—my first housewarming gift—on the back porch, I returned to the kitchen and picked up the phone. Anita's notation read "Rarity @ The Rare Curl."

Chapter Four

Tinkling chimes sounded as I pushed open the glass door of The Rare Curl and stepped into the reception area. Bright white side walls were covered with glass shelves stacked with bottles of shampoo, hairspray, and I couldn't guess what else. I stick with simple when it comes to my hair.

A curvy white desk occupied the center of the room, and there was a woman leaning over it, presumably the receptionist. Her face was concealed by a mass of curly red hair, but she swung the ringlets back when she looked up to greet me. I was startled by her bright green eyes surrounded by a maze of crinkly lines, and her enormous smile.

She nearly sang out, "Welcome. How may I help you today?"

"Hi, I'm Lauren Halloren. I called yesterday."

I realized I was still standing just inside the door, and forced myself to approach the desk.

She straightened and reached across the desk to

grab my hand, giving it a firm squeeze before releasing me. "I'm pleased to meet you, Lauren Halloren. I'm Rarity Peabody, proprietor. I'm betting you are Lauren Grace, Ruth James's niece. Welcome home."

"Yes, that's me."

Everybody knows Aunt Ruth.

"We heard you'd be living in Ruth's old place. It's such a nice house." Her voice, through her constant smile, continued to resonate with musical notes. "My gentleman friend, Wallace Binion, is your neighbor on the south side, in the white house. How are you getting settled into your new home?"

"I'm doing fine. I met Mr. Binion when I was moving in. He helped me unload."

"Oh, good. I'm glad he's being neighborly."

She beckoned me to a large arched doorway behind the desk. It opened to a room housing styling stations and chattering women.

Rarity pointed toward the first styling chair in a row of three. "Let's get you started. I'm right over here. Follow me."

I almost bumped into her when she stopped short and turned to face me. "Oh, dear, I heard you had some excitement in your neighborhood yesterday. Those thieves again. If it were me, I would have just let them run, but Clive is a hot-head. Imagine, shooting at them. But don't worry about him. He and Murine usually keep to themselves."

"Hmm, about the prowlers, why don't I ask Wallace to come over and make sure your house is secure? He's a whiz at security. When we started keeping company, he insisted I replace my locks. And then he made me start using them."

Rarity stepped aside and put her hand on the back of the styling chair. I took a seat before cocking my head to look up at her. "I think my locks are good. But thanks."

"Knowing Wallace, he probably talked Ruth into better locks, too."

Rarity rested a hand on my shoulder. "I sure miss her. It was a sad day for this town when she passed. She was quite a lady. The dear spent her time helping people, right up until the Good Lord took her home."

"I hadn't seen her in a long time." It was getting embarrassing that everyone knew my aunt better than I ever did.

I ran my hands through my hair. "Um…. I need a trim. It hasn't been cut for a while."

"You are in the right place." She whipped a cape into the air. It floated around me and gently settled into place.

"I just want it shaped up a bit. Not too short." A new hairdresser is enough to give me heart palpitations.

Rarity shoved her fingers into my hair and pushed it from side to side. Then she examined my head from every angle. She held a strand and studied it, finally saying, "Oh sure, I could give it some shape and trim off the bad ends."

She stared intently at my reflection in the mirror. "Do you wear bangs? You would look great with some hair on your forehead. You know, soft shadow bangs, swept to the side?"

"Do you think so?" I asked her reflection. "I haven't worn any for a while, but that might be nice."

She answered my reflection. "Okay. Let's do that. You can wear them down or brush them back out of the way. They'll be great. Let's get your hair washed."

I thought I might be lulled to sleep during the shampoo, but remained wide awake when we returned to the chair for the haircut. Scissors snipped wildly, and scraps of hair flew in all directions. All with Rarity talking nonstop.

A moderately chubby hairdresser, who'd been working next to us, cashed-out her customer and returned to flop into her chair, instantly joining our conversation. Rarity introduced her as Stacy Lutz and pointed out Patsy Clooney, working toward the back of the salon. Patsy looked up and waved.

The muscles of my face froze into what I hoped was a smile as I studied Stacy. Her hair had been clipped short in the back and over one ear, much longer on the other side. Long, spiky, pieces hung over one eye. I stared in horror at her reflection in the mirror. My pulse began to race and my breath came in short gasps. I couldn't seem to look away, but when I forced a glance at my own more conservative style, my blood pressure dropped to a normal rhythm.

"This is looking nice, Rarity."

Thank you God, it's going to be okay.

Rarity placed her scissors on the counter top and I relaxed. The scary part was over. She slopped on some mousse, grabbed a brush, and flipped on the blow dryer.

"Rarity," I raised my voice above the noise, "I wonder if you can recommend an antique dealer. There are a few items in the house I think may be worth something. I don't know anything about antiques so I'd like to have them appraised."

"Yes, Ruth had some beautiful glassware and furniture. They're family heirlooms. She treasured the memories they held. You're wise to have them appraised. I don't know anyone off-hand, but I'll ask around for a recommendation."

Rarity stepped back, accidentally colliding with Patsy. "Oops excuse me, Patsy. I didn't see you there." Patsy, now finished with her customer, was working around my chair with the broom, sweeping up all the hair clippings. She finished there and moved over to sweep Stacy's area as well.

"Thank you, girlfriend." Stacy lazily popped a piece of gum in her mouth.

Once upon a time, Patsy must have been beautiful. Her prominent cheekbones and large eyes were evidence of that. Today, puffy, dark arcs hung beneath her eyes and her hair had the straw-like appearance of too much hair dye.

Stacy eyed me. "Honey, did you see I Can Sing last night? My favorite TV show. I thought they were too hard on that Shaun. You know the little guy from Wisconsin?"

"I don't watch it."

Stacy went on as if I hadn't said anything. "He's so good. Has a beautiful voice. I vote for him every week.

You know you can text your vote in."

Rarity joined the conversation, commenting on the other contestants as the blow dryer whirred.

Patsy carried the broom to the back of the salon, and Stacy lowered her voice. "That Patsy is a gem. She's been sweeping up my hair every day for the last two weeks, bless her heart. Too bad that husband of hers doesn't appreciate what he's got."

She leaned forward, dropping her voice to a whisper. "He's never home. Patsy says he works a lot, but I think he's having an affair. She's so gullible."

"Now Stacy, you don't know that." Rarity chided.

"But Rarity, I'm pretty sure he's seeing that woman, Helen. She works at the nursing home, a new customer of mine. You know. The one who insists on bleaching her hair herself. I could tone it down and make her look years younger. Anyway, she was telling me about Earl selling her insurance, but if you ask me, she knows entirely too much about Earl to be just a business acquaintance."

Patsy emerged from the back room, and Stacy instantly returned her conversation to a detailed rundown of I Can Sing contestants. I don't think she paused to take a breath until Rarity finished my hair and removed the cape.

Rarity and I walked to the reception desk. As I paid, she leaned toward me and looked into my eyes. "I apologize for the gossip. I don't like unkind talk in the salon. It doesn't do anybody any good."

She opened the cash register, and recited, "Think on such things that are true and noble. Think about what is pure, what is lovely, and admirable. Think about things that are excellent and praiseworthy." It's from Philippians 4:8. I can't remember it word for word but I'm pretty sure it means don't gossip.

"Sounds like it to me. Thanks, Rarity. My hair is going to be great."

I left The Rare Curl thinking I looked kind of cute with the dubious bonus of knowing all about the I Can Sing contestants and the local gossip.

Chapter Five

The old tin mailbox overflowed. While I pulled out a handful of junk mail, a whisper soft sound caught my attention.

"Mew."

I scanned the area around the porch. Nothing. But there at my feet, a small, black and white cat looked up at me with huge golden eyes.

How sweet.

Then, in an instant, the cat's mouth gaped open and released an ear-piercing screech.

"Whoa, kitty. What a big voice you have. It's nice of you to stop by, but go on home now."

With my luck, he belonged to Clive. I sneaked a look at the blue house to confirm no one was watching, before I nudged the animal with the toe of my shoe.

"Shoo. Shoo."

He flattened himself on the concrete, becoming unmovable. With a little more pressure I rolled him over until there was enough space to open the door and squeeze through. I wasted no time pulling it closed.

"Sorry cat, it's time I get serious about writing. The move put me behind schedule. If I don't finish and send off a couple of articles, I won't be able to afford even this free house." I looked around and snapped my mouth shut. I was speaking to a cat, through a closed door.

Small town life had already muddled my mind.

In the kitchen, I loaded the coffee pot, set it on brew, and then crept to the door to peek out. No sign of the cat.

Coffee and writing consumed the remainder of the day. That and wishing I were more creative.

Several hours after I'd turned on the lamps, wind-whipped rain tapped against the window panes. Lightning strobed outside and a clap of thunder shook the house. I couldn't resist tiptoeing to the front window to scan the porch. Much to my dismay, a ball of black and white fur filled the corner beside the flower pot.

Wet patches began to form on the porch and I called through the door. "Go home kitty. You're going to get soaked."

The small head swiveled in my direction, ears turned down like a wide brimmed rain hat. There was no escaping the accusation in his golden eyes.

Shoot.

Why should I feel guilty because someone left their cat outside in the rain? It's not my cat.

"Dumb animal." I stomped to the closet to retrieve an empty box and pulled a garbage bag over it to repel water. On my way to the door, I thought to grab an old towel from the linen closet and tucked it inside the box.

Rain sprinkled my face as I pushed the cat out of the way and shoved the box between the flower pot and the house.

The feline gazed up at me, then at the box, and then stretched his neck to peer through the open door.

"Nope. No way. This is the best I can do for you. I can barely take care of myself. Get in the box or go back where you came from."

The cat stared at me, and I stared at him, neither one of us blinking until a gust of wind pelted us with rain drops. The cat wisely stepped inside the shelter of the box. I retreated into the house, turned off the lights, and took a book to bed.

Sometime in the night the sound of thumping drug me out of a sound sleep. Straining to locate the source was useless. All I could hear was the sound of my own heart beating. Laying still and slowing my breathing helped to quiet my nerves.

Thumping, scratching. Branches. Tree branches were being blown against the siding.

It's just the storm.

Chapter Six

Sunrise turned the fading clouds to pale peach with the promise of a beautiful day. I surveyed the storm damage. A few leaves and broken branches littered the lawn. Water had blown onto the back porch leaving small puddles on the floor. The puddles were in an interesting pattern. Almost like footsteps, I thought. But I was being silly. It was the wind. I mopped up the water and went to my computer, determined to work.

My day remained uninterrupted until the phone rang at five o'clock. Pushing away from the desk, it took me a minute to straighten up and limp to the phone. Sore, stiff muscles hindered movement.

"Hello, Lauren?" The greeting came through the receiver so loud I had to pull the phone away from my ear. "It's Clair. How are you, girl? I couldn't believe it when Anita told me you were back in town."

I carried the phone to the sofa and sat down. "Clair, it's good to hear from you. I'm working on getting settled. What have you been up to? Anita told me you're in real estate. With your energy, that sounds like the perfect career."

"We'll catch up on everything soon. Watcha doin' right now? Anita and I are on our way over with a bottle of wine, cheese, and a box of crackers. We should be there in fifteen minutes."

"No. What do you mean you're on your way?"
"We are. Can't wait to see you. Don't worry about cleaning up. It's just us."

Eek.

My heart sank as I scrutinized my cluttered living space. "I've been writing all day. There's a deadline this week and …."

"Then, it's about time you had a break. Gotta go, Anita took my keys and is already in the car. See you soon."

The phone went dead and I studied the living room. I hopped to my feet, picked up a magazine, and shoved it under some books on the shelf. I plucked my sweatshirt off the chair, ran it to the laundry basket, gathered and stacked stray papers on the desk, just in time to answer the door.

That was a quick fifteen minutes.

Clair hadn't changed much since high school. She still wore her hair darker than her natural light brown. It was still cut very short, but instead of curled, now stood out in pointy spikes. She was still slender, maybe even thinner than in school. Her flawless make-up, blazer, short skirt, and high heels revealed the business woman she'd become.

Clair shrieked. "Lauren, look at you. You haven't changed a bit. Still beautiful, even without make-up."

Have I combed my hair today? Had I showered?

After a quick but firm hug, Clair stepped past me and teetered toward the kitchen, holding a wine bottle above her head. "Where are the glasses? Let's get this party going."

Anita trailed in behind Clair, carrying a grocery bag. She leaned toward me and whispered. "Clair may have started without us, I'm driving. Sorry we're invading your space, but I think the three of us need to catch up." She winked and walked straight to the kitchen.

I closed the door and watched Clair opening and shutting cupboard doors.

When she sang out, "Ta-da." I knew she'd found what she was looking for. She pulled out three glasses and pointed Anita to the plates.

My space had not only been invaded, it had been taken captive and was about to be carried away. I threw my hands up in surrender and plopped down on the sofa while the two women carried in glasses filled to the brim and a plate piled with squares of cheese, and crackers.

Before long, Clair had us laughing at memories of high-school. She stopped mid-laugh and creased her brow. "What am I sitting on?" Leaning to one side, she pulled my book from under her hip.

"Oh. Sorry, I forgot that was there. I was reading it last night."

She made a face when she read the title. "Texas

<u>Greed and Murder</u>. Isn't this about the man who killed his wife for her inheritance?"

"Yes, that's the one. I'm addicted to true crime novels. Love detective stuff, trying to figure who did it before the author tells me."

"Ick. Not me. Give me a good romance anytime." Clair dropped the book on the side table and went back to her reminiscing.

The wine bottle was almost empty when I found myself telling of that dreadful day five years ago. "Sometimes I think if the phone hadn't rung, if only I hadn't answered it, life would be different. I was in the kitchen making Marc's favorite lasagna. I picked up the receiver, still stirring the sausage. I thought it was a bad joke. Marc and his buddy Jeff could sometimes come up with some terrible pranks, particularly after a day of fishing and beer. They thought they were hilarious. But this time, Jeff's voice sounded odd, out of breath, as though he had just run a marathon."

My lungs had run out of air and I sucked in a breath. "He told me Marc had been shot. A drive by. He said he was coming to get me, but I said no. I had to get to the hospital. That's when he told me to wait for him because Marc had already been pronounced dead."

Tears stung my eyes. "He blurted it out. Just like that. I dropped the phone and ran for the car. Everything after that is a blur. I don't remember driving to the hospital." I stared at the tissue Anita had put in my hand. "I barely remember being there. You know what's strange? I can still remember the smell of the sausage browning in the pan but I don't remember the funeral." I choked in oxygen.

Clair reached over and poured the remainder of the wine into my glass. Her mascara was smudged. I glanced at Anita. She held a tissue to her eyes.

I took time to breathe, and we sat in silence for a full minute. "I guess I put a damper on the evening."

Anita reached over and took my hand. "No Sweetie, you needed to tell the story. It's the only way to heal. But why didn't we know about this? Why didn't you come home?"

"I don't know why you didn't hear. Jeff took care of all the arrangements. He even called my father. Dad didn't come down for the funeral. I never even heard from him or from Aunt Ruth. I guess they were still mad I'd eloped. That's when I knew I was on my own. I didn't hear anything from them until three years ago when I got the notice that Dad died."

Clair huffed, and her voice rose to a higher pitch. "What? I can't believe they didn't go to be with you. And they didn't let any of us know. We would've been there."

Anita slapped the table, causing Clair and me to jump. "Wait a minute. Five years. Wasn't that about the time your father was diagnosed with Alzheimer's?"

I stared at Anita. "Alzheimer's? I never heard that. I got a note from Aunt Ruth that he'd been cremated because he was emaciated from an illness. I didn't even know there had been an illness."

"Oh gosh, Lauren. I'll bet it was at the same time. Your dad's mind was gone by then, so if Jeff called and talked to him, he wouldn't have remembered. Ruth wouldn't have heard of it. And poor Ruth had her hands full, taking care of him until she put him in Beaver Creek Nursing Home. She probably never thought to call you or maybe didn't know how to get hold of you. We wondered why you didn't come home then."

A rock formed in my stomach. "Or, if she did call, I didn't answer the phone. I was worthless for months. After a while, even my friends in Florida stopped calling."

Clair sniffed, "I'm dumbfounded. Your father gets Alzheimer's and Marc dies at the same time? What a horrible, horrible cosmic joke."

"I can't wrap my mind around this." I leaned against the sofa to rest my head, and closed my eyes.

I don't know how much time had passed when I opened them again. The house was dark, with only a single light shining from the kitchen. A blanket had been placed over me, and the plates and glasses had been cleared. I turned on a light and checked the door. My friends had locked it behind them.

In the morning, my head was foggy from the wine, but a weight was lifted from my shoulders. I'd shared the horror of Marc's death and survived. I'd learned a tragic turn of events had left me alone in my time of need. My father hadn't abandoned me and maybe, neither had Aunt Ruth.

Chapter Seven

The small air conditioner unit struggled, rendering the house a sauna, so I sat on the back porch hoping to catch a late morning breeze. The roar of Wallace's lawn mower drowned out any bird songs. My hairdresser, Rarity, sat at his picnic table gesturing to him as he mowed. Her mouth moved but was I willing to bet Wallace couldn't hear a word. He nodded at her and smiled as he pushed the mower on the far side of the yard.

Rarity caught sight of me, cupped her hand to the side of her mouth and called, "Lauren, how about a nice glass of lemonade? Wallace can't hear a thing I say to him with that mower running. I'll be right over."

She ran into Wallace's house and was back out in a flash.

After climbing my steps, and nudging the screen door open with her hip, she held out a large glass. "Fresh squeezed." Then she giggled. "Not by me. That's what it said on the bottle—all natural, fresh squeezed."

I gripped the glass, slippery with condensation. "This is wonderful, Rarity." The icy cold lemonade made my mouth pucker. "Thank you. It's perfect."

Rarity sat in the chair next to me and tucked her feet up underneath her. "This is such a nice porch. Ruth used it a lot in the last years."

I took in a deep breath. Time for the truth. Who was Aunt Ruth, the woman I remembered or the perfectly sweet lady these people talked about?

"Did she? I know you have such nice things to say about her, everyone does, but I remember a very strict, and not very kind, woman."

Rarity tipped her head to the side for a moment. "You're right. I think she was unhappy when you were young. I didn't know her well until after you'd moved away and your father had begun to show signs of dementia. She spent every day at his place, taking care of him. She changed a lot during that time. I think the stress transformed her. After he died, she'd become a much gentler person."

We drank our lemonade in silence a few minutes before Rarity continued. "You know, sometimes it's in the middle of a storm we realize we need help. And sometimes, it isn't until the storm's passed that we look back and see God's provision. I don't know exactly when it happened, but she found an inner peace. I saw it in her face."

Rarity reached out and touched my arm. "After that, Ruth always wanted to help the less fortunate, volunteering at the nursing home and the church. That woman found joy in every moment. She told me once she'd spent her life worrying about silly things. She didn't want to waste another minute."

"I'm surprised she wanted to help others after caring for my dad. It seems like she would want time for herself."

"That's what often happens when someone recognizes how God has helped them through a hard time. The gratefulness makes them want to share. Don't get me wrong. She enjoyed her life, too. She had the whole interior of the house painted in these pretty soft colors."

Rarity pointed at the frame hanging on the wall. "Did you know she painted that lovely inspirational verse herself? 'The trees of the field shall clap their hands.' Doesn't it make you smile? It's from the Old Testament."

"That's such a whimsical thought, perfect for this porch. I wish I had known that Aunt Ruth." I fell silent as I looked around the small porch, something pricking the back of my mind.

When my attention returned to Rarity, she was studying me. "I'm sorry. I got distracted. I was sure I put some flowers out here. They were in a really pretty pot. My friend Anita gave it to me."

"Perhaps you put it on the front porch."

"I don't think so. I must have left it in the house, maybe the kitchen." I pressed the cold glass against my hot forehead and laughed. "I must be losing it."

Rarity put her feet down and sat up straight. Pushing a stray curl from her face, she announced, "You're going to think I'm crazy, but I just had a thought. There are two or three mornings every week the girls and I are really busy at the salon. We hardly have time to think straight with trying to do hair while greeting customers, and answering the phone. Why don't you come and be my receptionist?"

That got my attention. "Me? I can use the extra income, but most of my time is dedicated to writing."

"It would be just Tuesday, Thursday, and Saturday. Say, from eight until noon? We'd love the help at the desk during the busy times. Yesterday morning, I was so busy I didn't know which way was up."

"I'd thought of getting a job. Do you think I could do it? I went through all kinds of odd jobs in Florida, but I don't know anything about hair."

"You don't have to know about hair, and I can teach you how to schedule appointments. Pretty much, all you have to do is be nice to the customers. The hardest thing is staying calm when one of the hairdressers throws a hissy-fit. But don't worry about that. I'll run interference until you get used to them."

Rarity's smile grew bigger than ever. Curls bobbed and the ice rang like bells, as she waved her glass in the air. "Oh, say you will. God must have arranged this. He knew I needed help and here you are."

I couldn't help but laugh along with her. I certainly could use some extra money. Maybe things were looking up. Maybe God did arrange it.

"Okay, I'll try it. When do you want me to start?"

"The sooner, the better. Can you come tomorrow? I'm not busy in the morning so we can work at scheduling appointments. Oh, this is going to be fun."

Rarity leaned over and hugged me. "I'm so excited."

Chapter Eight

Birds were singing the next morning, as I hopped into the Chrysler to head to The Rare Curl, for my first day of work. It's amazing what the promise of a little extra money will do for my attitude. A paycheck would ease my financial worries and get me out of Evelynton even faster.

Rarity met me at the door and took me straight to the front desk for a quick lesson on scheduling. She'd made up a cheat-sheet, listing the timing and cost of services. Within twenty minutes, I was fielding calls on my own.

Stacy hurried in carrying a large box of donuts. "Rarity called and told me you would be here. Welcome, girlfriend. These will be in the break room when you want one."

Patsy slipped in quietly, glanced at me when I said "Hello" and proceeded to the back of the salon.

During the first two hours, I'd had time for coffee and a donut, scheduled five appointments, and calmed a customer when Stacy got off schedule. I was beginning to think this might be my perfect job.

I'd just replaced the handset on the phone when the door opened, and a pale, twig of a woman crept in.

"Good morning. How may I help you?"

Her voice was little more than a whisper. "Patsy." She padded past me so quietly that I couldn't resist glancing down to see if she was wearing bedroom slippers. She wasn't—they were regular shoes. She slithered into the chair where Patsy waited, cape in the air.

The woman seemed familiar. I was willing to bet she'd been the one who'd watched me on the day I moved in, from the upstairs window of the blue house.

I ran a finger down Patsy's column in the appointment book until I found the woman's name— Murine Baron—and decided to speak to her on her way out. However, before long, I looked up to see Murine open the front door.

"Murine...." Too late. She was gone.

Patsy hovered at my shoulder and handed me a check. "This is for Murine." The check was signed in a bold signature, Clive Baron. His was the only name on the account. The address was 416 Stoneybridge.

I swiveled my chair around. "Patsy," I said, catching her as she turned to go to her styling station. "Murine is my neighbor. I wish I'd caught her before she left. I was hoping to introduce myself."

Patsy half turned toward me and put her hand on her hip. "She's shy. You probably would have scared her half to death. She hardly talks to me, let alone strangers. Her husband is a friend of Earl's." She wagged a finger in my direction, nodding. "You're the one."

With that, she retrieved a broom from the corner and returned to her chair.

I'm the--? "Patsy, wait. What did you mean by 'You're the one'?"

Patsy's brows rose when she turned toward me again. "Oh, nothing. Just that you're the one who moved in." She paused for a minute. "Clive's not the friendliest guy. He wanted your house for his son and thought he could buy it cheap when Ruth died. He wouldn't have been happy with anyone except Clive Jr. moving in. He acts mean, but don't worry about him." Patsy went back to her chair.

Sure. I shouldn't worry about a big gruff man who's mad at me and keeps a loaded 12 gauge.

I was studying the appointment book later when Rarity came to the desk and put her hand on my shoulder. "You did a great job today, Lauren. You're a natural. How did you like it?"

I glanced at the clock, thinking twelve noon never looked so good. I'd worked my full four hour shift. What would I do if I had to work a full day?

"I'm finished for the day? The time went fast. It was fun."

Okay, I was stressed and tired, but no need to tell my boss. I had my handbag on my shoulder before I finished speaking.

"I could tell you were enjoying your work. You are good with the customers. So, I'll see you day after tomorrow?"

I was half-way to the door when I waved. "Sure thing. I'll see you Saturday morning." The phone rang and Rarity answered it.

I stepped out onto the sidewalk, and breathed a sigh of relief.

Chapter Nine

'd parked the Lincoln two block down the street, and on my way there, I passed a storefront where fluttering caught my eye. Inside, Anita and Clair pressed their faces to the window. They waved and motioned for me to come inside.

On the glass above them, bold letters read Ava's Java Shop. A coffee shop. Why hadn't I noticed it before?

The aroma of freshly brewed coffee engulfed me as soon as I pushed through the door. The upscale decor surpassed my expectations for a small town shop. The walls were mouthwatering tones of milk chocolate and latte, the counters and tables a deep coffee brown, and overstuffed chairs in varying shades of forest green.

"We're over here, Lauren." Clair's voice rose above the chatter.

"Coming." I wandered to their table, taking in the pewter lighting fixtures. "This place is fabulous."

"It's our favorite." Clair scooted her chair out as I sank into mine. "I'm buying your first cup of Ava's amazing coffee. Or would you like one of the special coffee drinks? Caramel java macchiato?"

"No. Thank you, straight with a little cream would be wonderful."

Clair's heels clicked as she trotted toward the counter.

I turned to Anita. "This is great. I love it. Reminds me of home—well, Florida."

Anita added a packet of sugar to her cup and stirred. "We always meet here. You'll have to join us."

She tapped a notebook sitting open in front of her. "This is the final meeting of the reunion committee. The cocktail party is tomorrow. You're coming, aren't you? Drinks and snacks. It'll be fun."

I grimaced. "Yikes. I forgot. Maybe I'll stop by for a while. You know me and crowds."

Anita picked up her cup and peered over the top. "I know, but I also know that once you're there, you'll have fun."

Clair reappeared, and slid an emerald green ceramic mug in front of me." Ava's special blend. It's the best."

"Thank you." I let the hot liquid roll down my throat. My eyes closed, and I almost purred. "Excellent."

When I opened my eyes, Clair was back in her chair, wide-eyed and staring at something over my left shoulder. I turned to follow her gaze until I found the focus of her attention. Ava was handing a brown to-go cup to a tall man with broad shoulders. I recognized the dark hair, and when he turned, I remembered the dark eyes from my first day in Evelynton. His gaze crossed mine, and I caught the hint of a smile before he turned his attention to the exit. I might have imagined it since he seemed otherwise unconcerned with the three awe-struck women staring in his direction.

"Whoa," Clair said in an uncharacteristically soft voice. She turned her head and tracked him as he walked to the door, then craned her neck to peer through the window. She was silent as he climbed into a black SUV and drove away.

"Cute." Anita quipped, and looked back at her notes. "Do you think we ordered enough of those little sausages for the cocktail party?"

When no answer came, she looked up at Clair, whose attention was still riveted to the disappearing SUV.

"Clair. Snap out of it. Didn't you just tell me you were in love with that guy you met? You know, the one you've been seeing almost every night? Remember Philip? What's his last name?"

Clair turned to face us. "Townsend. Philip Townsend. And I am in love with him. I was only looking." Her gaze wandered back at the window. "Have you seen that beautiful man before? Wonder who he is."

"It's looking that lands you in trouble every time." Anita shook her head. "I've never seen him before."

Clair took a gulp of her coffee and directed her

attention to me. "How could I not admire him? He's gorgeous, isn't he Lauren?"

"Hmm. He was nice looking." I concentrated on my coffee, giving my best unimpressed performance.

"Well ladies, I think I should ask around. He's new in town and might want to buy a house. It's my business to know people." She tipped up her coffee mug, and drained the contents.

Anita leaned back and folded her arms across her chest. "Clair, you never change. When will you settle down?"

"Maybe with Philip, but I'll stop looking at gorgeous men when…." She shrugged and flapped her hand in dismissal. "I never will. Anyway, I'll find out who this one is. Trust me."

Clair shot out of her chair, and strode to the counter. Once she got Ava's attention, the two women put their heads together for a few minutes. My friend returned and pressed both hands on the table, smiling like the Cheshire cat. "Ava says he paid cash so she doesn't know his name, but he has something to do with the police department. She saw him go in there early this morning when she was on her way to work."

Clair picked up her handbag and phone. "Talk to you later, girls. I have a woman to see."

She tipped her head toward me. "My friend Irma does the filing at the police station. Bye, ladies."

Clair turned on her heel and strode toward the door.

Chapter Ten

Crumpled pages littered the sofa. I threw my pen across the room after scratching out yet another idea praising Hoosier snow. It was impossible to work up excitement for a story of an Indiana winter, something I remembered well, frigid temperatures, slippery roads, and shoveling snow.

A knock at the door was a welcome intrusion saving me from further frustration. I retrieved the pen on the way to answer it.

Clair stood on the porch, talking to the cat. "Hi, Clair. This is a nice surprise." She gave the cat a pat on the head and turned to come in. I let my friend pass before I stuck out my foot to block the furry tag-a-long. He sat back on his haunches and glared at me when his nose bumped the side of my shoe.

As I closed the door, Clair turned weary eyes to me and exhaled. "Coffee?"

"Of course. Have a seat in the dining room, and I'll join you for a cup. What's up?"

She was uncharacteristically quiet as I filled two mugs. I delivered hers, and sat across from her with mine. "Are you okay?"

Clair leaned in with her elbows on the table. "I'm fine. I was in the neighborhood and thought I'd stop in to remind you about tonight."

"Tonight?"

Crap. How easily I'd put it out of my mind, again.

"We're having cocktails and snacks at Wild Olive. This is the reunion warm-up for anyone who may be in town early, before the dinner tomorrow." Clair paused long enough to take a big drink of her coffee, and then pointed an index finger at me. "Seven o'clock, in the party room. I've already made your name tag."

Visions of a quiet evening in front of the television came to mind, so I put on my tired face. "I've been so busy, I thought I'd skip it. I'm on a deadline for a magazine article that's giving me fits and—"

Clair shook her head. "Uh-uh. Lauren, no excuses. You have to go. This is for your own good. Get out and mingle, make new friends."

She gripped the mug with both hands and lowered her voice. "Move on. That's what I'm doing."

Ha. I knew something had been troubling her. "What is it, Clair? You know everyone in town. What's going on?"

"Oh...." Clair's shoulders drooped a little and she suddenly became interested in a spot on the table. "I think it's over with Phillip."

"Over? Didn't we just talk about him yesterday?"

"Yeah, I know. I suspected it then but didn't want

to say anything."

Clair breathed in and straightened her shoulders. "When we first met, Philip wanted to be with me every day. He was almost possessive. Sent flowers, declared his love for me. The man couldn't stand the thought of us being apart. I felt like a queen."

She gave a sad laugh. "I let myself fall for him, and now for the last week, he's suddenly too busy for me. There must be another woman."

I put down my coffee in order to grasp her hand. "Clair, I'm so sorry. Are you sure? Maybe he has something going on at work."

She shook her head. "It isn't work. Every time I call him, he's very short with me. And yesterday, after I left Ava's, I saw him on the street. He was about a block away and I waved. He turned around and went the other way."

"Clair, I bet there's some other explanation."

"No. I called him. When he didn't pick up, I sent him a text. Later, he texted back claiming he hadn't seen me. Trust me, he did. I know it's over."

She took another deep breath and patted her perfect hair. "Another one bites the dust. More fish in the sea, as my mother said many times. So anyway, come to the party tonight. Do this for me because I need my best friends with me."

Okay. Okay. I could get over my aversion to crowds for my friend.

"Of course, I'll come."

Clair smiled and squeezed my hand. "Great, I'm so grateful. And you'll have fun, wait and see." She relaxed back in her chair. "I'm on my way home to change clothes. I have to be there early to finish setting up. See you about seven?"

"Sure, seven." I watched as she downed her coffee and pushed away from the table, and then walked with her to the door.

Clair came to an abrupt stop and turned to me. "Oh hey, I found out who that tall dark stranger is. You know, the guy at Ava's Java? Jack Spencer. Nobody seems to know much about him, except he's some kind of investigator, FBI, CIA, NCIS, ATF, or whatever. At last, a little excitement in E-town."

"Is he?" Law enforcement. Why are men in authority, in uniform—so to speak—so interesting? Too much television. In my experience, they haven't all been heroes.

"I don't know why he's in town. Irma, at the police department, said he was talking to Melvin, the police chief. They kept the door closed, and Melvin wouldn't tell her anything, so the info is all office gossip—but reliable."

"Fascinating. What would he have to investigate here in Evelynton?"

Clair chuckled. "Not much. Maybe he's lost. But I hope he sticks around."

She opened the door and stepped out. "What a pretty cat. Looks like she's wearing a little tuxedo. What's her name?"

"I don't know. It isn't my cat."

Clair tilted her head and wrinkled her brow. "She's not yours? Why does she have this little house?"

I sighed. "The cat was sitting out there in the rain, and I gave it the box to crawl into. But it's not my cat."

"Huh," Clair gave the cat a pat on the head and said good-bye to it. Then she waved at me and skipped down the steps.

"I'll see you later." I glanced at Wallace's before I shut the door. No black SUV, no car at all.

Back at my desk, plagued with poor concentration and non-existent creativity, I shut down my computer, and promised myself I'd write all day Saturday. I went to the bedroom, hoping my closet held something cute to wear.

By the time I'd showered, dressed, and finished drying my hair, it was seven o'clock. I was late, and I hate being late. I wanted to get to the restaurant, and find a secluded table before it got crowded.

In my rush out the door, I tripped over the feline, who still squatted on my porch. The cat hissed and skittered away in a mad dash for the bushes. Meanwhile, my arms flailed in many directions, in hopes my hands would land on something to break my fall. I finally found the railing and latched on, saving me from a tumble down the steps. Straightening, I pushed my hair out of my face and muttered a few words that would have shocked Aunt Ruth.

Chapter Eleven

Deep cleansing breaths. In. And out. In. And out. I smoothed my hair and tried to appear calm and collected—as if I hadn't just done a sprint through the Wild Olive parking lot. I entered the room quietly, remaining inconspicuous and unnoticed, until Clair spotted me.

"Lauren, I'm so glad you came! Look at you. So glamorous." She couldn't have attracted more attention if she'd sounded a trumpet and held up a sign.

The mob closed in, hugging, offering greetings, making introductions.

I barely remember these people. Why are they so happy to see me?

Too many people, too fast. My chest constricted and I took a couple of steps back, struggling to inhale. But I maintained a thin smile and returned salutations, while I peeked between shoulders, in search of my escape route.

My gaze fell on my friend sitting alone, picking at a plate of chicken wings.

I looked sincerely into the eyes of a blond, a cheerleader if I recall. "It's great to see you, but would you excuse me? There's Anita, I have to give her a message before I forget." I struggled through the group, excusing myself at every step, and ultimately claimed a chair against the wall. My heart rate began to settle to a normal rate.

"Help. I'm not sure I can handle all these gushing people. I don't even remember who they are."

Anita licked the tips of her fingers and wiped them on a napkin, before sliding a book toward me. "Here's the yearbook. Leaf through it to remind yourself of names and faces. Works for me."

"Great idea." I paged through to find the senior class, flipping first to our portraits. "Look how young we were. Oh, my hair was really fluffy. Why did I think that was attractive?"

Anita laughed. "Can you believe I wore all that eye makeup? Blue shadow, for goodness sake."

From the sanctuary of the table, I monitored the room as it continued to fill, attempting to match each arrival with a senior portrait.

Clair emerged from the crowd and placed a glass of wine in front of me. "You've been sitting ten minutes. Take this and go mingle. It's easier with something in your hand."

What would I do without friends to coach me on social skills? I took the glass and obediently mingled. I smiled at everyone's wonderful life, gushed at pictures of beautiful kids, and acted suitably impressed at their stories of a prosperous career. I noticed that although people said they wanted to reconnect, they mainly talked about themselves. Easier for me.

When the subject of Marc's death came up, condolences were short, and my classmates wandered away to find someone less depressing.

It took no thought, or scanning of the yearbook, to recognize Perry Sizemore as he made his entrance. Never a thin person, he was now a formidable presence. He glad-handed his way around the room and left each cluster of classmates laughing.

I stepped close to Clair. "Is Perry in politics?"

"No. Real estate. He's my competition. Look out, he's coming this way." Clair slipped away, leaving me stranded in his path. I felt like a steak sandwich under Perry's glassy-eyed gaze. Fortunately, at the last minute, a new arrival diverted his attention.

Perry executed a sharp left turn toward the door. "Hey Paul. You made it after all."

Perry threw his arm around the tanned, lean, man and guided him to the bar. The newcomer wasn't a classmate, nor was he a stranger. It was the runner I'd almost flattened with the van. A thought crossed my mind to give him a taste of my anger at his carelessness. I decided against it and scanned the room, wondering which woman had almost lost her husband that day.

Clair skipped to the runner—almost roadkill—and attached a name tag to his shirt. I edged forward and strained my eyes to decipher the name. Paul Cooper?

A classmate. I recalled the name but failed to place the face.

I stood back trying to picture him as a teen, without success. Anita edged up beside me and pulled me into the group where Perry was keeping everyone entertained. Nestled in behind Anita, I peered over her shoulder and searched Paul Cooper's facial features. I was baffled and then embarrassed because Paul caught me staring—twice.

"Sorry, Paul, I'm trying to remember everyone from high-school." I shook my head. "My memory. Guess I'm getting old."

Paul's gaze darted to my name tag and, just as quickly, returned to Perry.

Backing out of the group, I meandered to the yearbook and read names. *Cameron, Causely, Chapman, Cooper.* There he was, but I saw no resemblance between the seventeen-year-old and the adult Paul Cooper. Where was the innocent smile? And the straight nose?

Could it have been broken?

Clair startled me when she came up from behind. She set her drink down and leaned heavily on the table. "Whew. I have to take a break. How's it going?"

"It's going alright. I'm glad you convinced me to come."

I nodded in Paul's direction. "Paul Cooper should get some kind of prize. He's the most changed. I didn't recognize him, at all."

"Really? I thought you'd remember all the good looking men." She glanced over at him. "Although, he's more attractive now than in school."

"Honestly Clair, he could be a completely different person. It's as if I'm looking at a stranger." I tapped his picture with my index finger. "It's this Paul Cooper, right?"

"Yeah. That's the only one we have." She laughed—loudly. I knew I shouldn't have brought it up. Should have taken note of her alcohol consumption.

Clair made little quotation marks with her fingers. "It's the Mystery Woman." Another loud laugh. "You haven't changed a bit. You were the only kid in school who watched the evening news for fun. Always looking for clues."

Clair retrieved her glass, causing the liquid to swirl and barely stay within the rim. "Maybe he's an impostor, or could it be that it's really Paul, but he's had facial reconstruction. He probably committed a crime and doesn't want to be recognized. Not sure why he'd show up here and wear a name-tag, though." She laughed at her joke.

"Very funny, Clair. That doesn't even make sense."

I put my hands up in surrender. "I only said he should get the prize for most changed in appearance."

Clair lost interest in our conversation and pointed to the other side of the room. "I need to make sure they replenish the chicken wings. Talk to you later, Mystery Woman." She made a beeline for the food table exercising the strut of a runway model.

Anita soon filled the chair next to me and placed a plate of crackers and cheese dip on the table. "Having fun Lauren? You know more people than you thought, don't you?"

I examined my glass, wondering whether I should get a refill. "I do. I remember most of them." I hesitated. Maybe it would be best to let it go. But not yet. "You know, I can't remember Paul Cooper. I mean, I remember a Paul Cooper from school but in my memory, he doesn't resemble this guy." I peered at the crowd where Paul was standing, just as he looked my way. I jerked my eyes back to Anita.

"You've been away and it's natural to forget some people. Not many of us look like we did twenty-five years ago." She finished her cracker and reached up to pat her hair. "Some of us have adopted a few pounds and grown some gray hair."

I picked up a cracker and put it back on the plate. "But there are always traces." I pulled the yearbook over, still open to Paul's picture. "Look at him. Do you see any resemblance?"

"Sure." Anita leaned in for a better look. "Well, no. He has changed a lot." She pulled the book closer. "A lot. I have to admit he's held up better than most of the men here."

I popped the cracker in my mouth, sat back, and determined to forget about Paul Cooper.

Clair drifted by, leaving a trail of alcohol droplets in her wake. Anita waved at her. "Come and sit for a while. We have a question for you."

Clair made her way to the table and eased into the chair. "What is it, ladies?"

"Do you think Paul Cooper resembles his yearbook picture?" Anita pushed the book toward her.

"You too, Anita?" Clair once again erupted in laughter. She brought the picture very close to her face and giggled. "You're right." She pushed the book away and opened her eyes wide. "What if he's a spy? Right here in Evelynton, Indiana." She leaned toward us and whispered. "Maybe I should contact Mr. Beautiful—Jack Spencer, the FBI guy."

She straightened, lifted her chin, and looked down her nose at us. "No, I'm in charge here. I'll go right up and ask Paul who he really is. If he's an impostor, he doesn't have any right to be at our reunion." Clair pushed her chair out.

She began to rise, and I grabbed her arm. "Oh no. We were having fun, but I don't want to embarrass Paul by letting him know we're talking about him." In Clair's condition, everyone would know.

"Okay, girls. I'll keep your secret. Got to run to the little girl's room." Clair rushed off, her walk still impressively steady.

Anita tipped her head toward me. "That was close."

"No kidding." I wanted to let it go, but couldn't. "Did Paul stay in town after high-school?"

"No. He moved away right after graduation and came back five or six years ago. I think he worked in New York City." Anita yawned and shifted to a more comfortable position. "He quit that job, and now sells real estate with Perry. I'm surprised he showed up tonight. He and his wife, Missy, don't socialize much. She's not even here."

"Missy? Do I know her?" I extracted my attention

from Paul, at the other side of the room.

Anita shook her head. "No, Missy moved to town a few years ago. She met Paul and they hit it off right away. Got married about two months later."

I turned in my chair to face Anita. "Two months? Wow. Love at first sight."

Anita put her elbows on the table and rested her chin on one hand. "I know. Isn't it sweet?"

Paul wasn't in sight when I turned to scan the room. "It just seems odd that he looks like a stranger."

Anita patted my shoulder. "You were always the one to solve mysteries. If there was an inconsistency anywhere, you would find it. But I think you're obsessing about this one."

"I guess you're right."

My energy had faded. "I think I'm ready to call it a night."

"Me too. You and I were much better partyers in high-school."

"Fond memories, but now, crowds wear me out. Besides, I have work to do—a deadline to meet."

"Too bad I can't leave until everybody else does. I have to settle up with the restaurant, and drive Clair home."

"I wish I had your excuse. What are you writing?"

"An article for <u>Midwestern</u> Life."

Anita's eyebrows shot up. "<u>Midwestern Life</u>? That's so exciting."

"Not to me. Exciting would be a serious news article or a True Crime novel."

Maybe something about identity theft?

Time to call it a night. Paul Cooper, or whoever he was, had left the room.

Chapter Twelve

I pushed myself up on an elbow and squinted at the clock before reaching for the phone. Eight a.m. What crazy person would call me at this time of day?

What day was it?

"Good morning, Ms. Halloren. Earl Clooney here—with Justice Insurance Agency. Listen, I am really sorry to bother you on Saturday morning, but I'm so embarrassed. I wonder if you would rescue me. Somehow we missed signing a form when you were in the other day."

"A form?" I tried to clear my head and massaged my temple where a dull headache had begun to throb.

"Part of your house insurance packet. It's an important document and I don't know how I missed it. Might have been stuck to another page, I guess. But could I stop by this morning?"

"This morning?"

Wake up.

"You see, I'm only a few blocks from you. It would save me some ribbing from the guys at the main office if I could get it faxed in today."

"Umm. Okay."

"Great, I'll come right over. It will only take a minute for you to sign on the dotted line."

I fell back onto my pillow. "Well, give me ten minutes."

"Great. See you soon." The phone went dead. I stared at the ceiling. Why did I tell him he could come?

I crawled out of bed and tugged sweats on over my pajamas.

It had been far less than ten minutes when the knock
rattled the door—just long enough to make coffee. I pressed the warm mug to my forehead as I shuffled to answer it.

"Good morning, Lauren."

Why was he shouting? He'll wake the neighbors.

"Morning, Mr. Clooney." I struggled to raise my voice above a whisper.

"Call me Earl. We're old friends now." He followed me to the living room and pulled up a side chair. "Beautiful day out there."

I collapsed on the sofa. Earl took his sweet time pulling the form from a folder, before handing it to me.

"I can't tell you how much I appreciate this."

"No problem." I scribbled my name on the line marked with an X and pasted a smile on my face when I passed it back to him. "There you go. I'm glad I could help." Retrieving my coffee, I got to my feet and led

73

the way to the door.

"Yep. It's a gorgeous day. Just look at that sun." His smile was becoming infuriating. "You have a good day now, little lady."

He stepped outside but turned back before his foot hit the first step. "Careful with that caffeine. It's a killer." He winked at me and then continued to his car.

"Uh huh."

This caffeine is the only thing that saved your life today, Earl.

The sofa beckoned me once more, but as I snuggled into the cushions, reality sent a wakeup call. It was Saturday. Rarity would be expecting me at work.

Oh crap.

Chapter Thirteen

Finished. I clicked the Send button to email the article to the editor. The muscles in my back screamed when I stood up, stiffened by eight hours of sitting—four at The Rare Curl reception desk and four more at my computer here at home. I kneaded a knot in my aching neck and turned to consider the weather. Trees, framed by the window, were bent in the wind and silhouetted against a slate sky. A good night to stay home. Clair and Anita expected me at the reunion, but I longed for the sofa and a movie.

The sofa would have won, except the image of Paul Cooper popped into my brain. Is it weird I've always loved a mystery?

I ran—half hobbled—for the shower. Forty-five minutes later, I climbed into the car.

Rain pounded the windshield as I trolled the crowded parking lot, up one row and down another. The only available spot was at the back, and I splashed through puddles in my dash for the restaurant.

Clair found me catching my breath under a huge banner that read Welcome Class of '89. "Lauren! You're just in time. Look at the buffet. It's a feeding frenzy."

She pushed me into line and put a dinner plate in my hands.

A voice rose above the clatter of dishes. "Lauren James. How are you? Gorgeous as ever, I see."

"Perry, you're a flatterer. How's Marlene?"

I busied myself in choosing the perfect chicken breast.

"She's fantastic. Working tonight." Perry Sizemore chose both roast beef and chicken, before turning his attention to a bowl heaped with mashed potatoes. "Wow, nice spread."

Clair and I carried our plates to join Anita. As Clair settled into her chair, she perused the crowd and chirped, "Oh Paul, here's an empty chair. Come and talk to us." She shifted her gaze and shot me a lopsided grin. He sat two seats away, and she raised her voice. "Paul, do you remember Lauren? She moved back home a few weeks ago."

A polite smile crossed his face. "Of course. We spoke last night. How are you, Lauren?"

I put down my fork. "I was disappointed we didn't have time to talk more. I'd love to hear what you did after high school. Someone mentioned you were out of state until a few years ago. Where did you live?"

As if he hadn't heard me, Paul turned his attention to the far end of the table. "Perry, how's the sale of that property on Yellowwood Road going?"

My mouth fell open.

That was rude.

"Fabulous. I finally got the seller and buyer to agree." Perry's face flushed as he recounted the negotiations.

Perry paused to breathe and I asserted myself. "Paul, tell me about your life after high school. Where did you go?"

Paul froze, his fork poised an inch from his mouth. He plastered on a phony smile.

Was I imagining that?

"College. Then I fell into the rat race and spent my time trying to get ahead, like everyone else."

I held his gaze. "How did that go? What company did you work for?"

He waved his fork at me, with enough force I was afraid the food might dislodge. "That part of my life isn't even worth mentioning. I got fed up and left." His chest expanded with a breath and his face softened. "I moved back to Evelynton, met Missy, and life changed."

I sat up straighter, glancing around. "Your wife? I'd love to meet her."

His fork clanged onto his plate. "She's home with a cold. Perry talked me into making an appearance, but I should be getting back." He lifted his wrist in an obvious display of checking the time.

"Oh, you haven't even finished your meal." I searched for more questions. "Didn't someone say you were in New York? How did you like the city?"

The softness vanished and his tone turned cross. "Yeah, I was there. I didn't like it. As I said, I don't talk about it." Voices hushed for a few seconds. I returned my attention to my plate and picked at a few green beans. New conversations began around the table.

Another bright idea popped into my mind. "I wish I had my camera." Ignoring Anita's raised eyebrows I went on. "I have to get some pictures. Oh wait, my cell phone."

"It's here somewhere." I dug through my bag, finally laying hands on the phone as I heard a chair scrape the floor. "Found it." I pulled it out in time to see Paul edging into the crowd and snapped a quick photo. The picture caught him in profile. I jumped up, and with Paul in the background, aimed at Clair and Anita, snapping several pictures in rapid succession.

"We didn't have time to pose." Clair glared at me. "I had food in my mouth."

"You looked great, but I'll take another." Clair and Anita put their heads together and smiled, and I snapped a couple. This time, Paul had vanished.

Dinner lost its appeal and the swirls of conversation blurred. I'd been obnoxious, but Paul hadn't given me a direct answer. He never said what he did after high school or where he worked. He got angry. What was that about?

Suddenly exhausted, I picked up my bag and slipped out of the room.

Chapter Fourteen

A drenching rain continued relentlessly during my drive home. Oncoming headlights reflected at odd angles on the wet pavement, obscuring landmarks, and throwing unnerving shadows.

My little house on Stoneybridge appeared at last, and I parked the Chrysler safely in the drive. I pulled my collar close, ducked my head, and ran up the sidewalk.

The door swung open as soon as I turned the key, and a damp breeze whistled through. The house was cold, and my search for an open window stopped short at the kitchen. A black and white cat sat in the middle of the checkered linoleum floor.

"How did...? Oh, I see." The back door stood open. Must have forgotten to lock it and the wind blew it open. I scolded myself internally while wind-milling my arms and shouting "Shoo, shoo." This proved effective in herding the kitty to the porch. I opened the screen door and he slunk out. "Good night, cat."

~

"Two, three, four." Teaspoons of coffee grounds went into the pot. A good night's sleep had cleared my thoughts and reminded me of priorities. My imagination had run away from me and I'd been distracted from the goal. I determined to stop wasting my time, pay off debt, and leave this Podunk town.

How much would Aunt Ruth's antique vases bring? I opened the cupboard. Empty shelves.

The glassware had to be there. Possibly they had been shoved to the back. But when I reached in, my hand landed on bare wood. Opening the next cupboard, and then the next, I found only cheap dishes and canned goods. A jog to the one cupboard in the dining room revealed only table cloths and place mats.

A gloomy mist settled into my heart. It had to have been a robbery. I dashed to the bedroom and pulled open the top dresser drawer. My wedding ring remained securely hidden in the back, wrapped in a sock. I opened other drawers and turned to the closet. Clothes were mussed and out of place, but nothing was missing.

The police department took an irritating four rings to pick up. A woman's nasally voice drawled. "Evelynton Police Department."

By that time, my pulse was racing. "I need a policeman. I've been robbed and—"

"Stop right there. Start with your name." I pictured her chewing gum and searching for paper and pencil.

"Um, sorry." I calmed myself enough to give my name, address, and reason for calling.

She calmly assured me a patrolman would be

dispatched as soon as he came in. I wanted to ask "Come in from where?" but thanked her and hung up, with little confidence he would arrive anytime soon.

I climbed the stairs, trying to remember what I'd stored in the spare rooms. A cursory investigation revealed my few belongings intact, and a rapping downstairs announced the arrival of a policeman.

His uniform immaculate, his posture perfect, bare skin above his ears signaled a fresh haircut. He was probably a ten years younger than me, although his grim expression made him look old. "Good morning, ma'am. I'm Officer Farlow with the Evelynton Police Department."

He appeared more professional than I'd expected in Evelynton and I let out the breath I'd been holding. "I remember. You were next door a few days ago. My friend Anita spoke to you."

"Yes ma'am. Now about your call. We don't want to waste time, do we?"

"Sorry. Thank you for your quick response. Please come in."

I went to the sofa and pulled a blanket around my shoulders. Officer Farlow perched on the side chair and flipped open a notebook. "You say, you were robbed?"

"Yes. I came home last night, and the back door was open, and there was a cat in the kitchen." I glanced that way, visualizing the scene. "I didn't think anything of it at the time. I thought the wind blew the door open, but this morning I discovered there were things missing."

Officer Farlow kept his eyes on his notes as he

spoke. "You were out when you think the incident occurred?"

I sat up and pulled the blanket closer. "Yes. I was at my high school reunion and got home about nine o'clock."

"And that's when your cat was in the house and you discovered the theft?"

"Um. No. That's when I discovered the open door and the cat. It's not my cat, someone else's. It wasn't until this morning that I discovered the antique vases missing."

"Vases." He jotted a notation. "And what else?"

"As far as I know, that's all that was taken. I checked through the house and didn't notice anything."

computer sitting like that, in plain view, last night?" He glanced around the room. "And the television. It was there last night?"

Perplexed, I glanced at the items and back at Farlow. "Um, yes. I haven't moved anything."

"Ms. Halloren, electronic devices are the first things a thief picks up." He pointed his pen toward both items. "But these are still here."

I ran my hands through my hair, wishing I had a ponytail holder. "But they're old. Can't be worth much."

"They don't look old to me." Another notation in the notebook. "Can you describe the vases, you say were stolen? What kind were they?"

"Um, one was white with a hand painted design of a tree. At least, it looked hand painted. One was crystal. I think it's cut glass. And there was another one. I think that one was blue. All three were about this tall." I held one hand above the other, to indicate size. "I'm pretty sure they're antiques. I inherited them from my aunt, with the house, and I was going to have them appraised. That's why I looked for them this morning."

"Not much of a description." Farlow continued writing.

He flipped the notebook shut and stood. "Let's take a walk through the house. While I check it out, you can explain to me what you think happened."

"Okay." I reluctantly left the blanket on the sofa and led the way to the kitchen, pointing to the back door and the empty cupboard.

He inspected the porch and checked through all my kitchen cupboards before we toured the rest of the house. After taking a quick peek into the bedrooms and bathrooms, he led the way to the living room, where he turned to look me in the eye for the first time.

"Nothing else is missing? So, you think the perpetrator came in specifically for the vases?" He smirked. "This is a small town, Ms. Halloren. We don't usually run into criminals with a taste for glassware."

He sobered when I leveled my gaze at him. "Um. Who knew about these vases?"

"Nobody. Or, I don't know who would know about them. I guess anyone who knew my aunt. I don't know that the thief came just for the vases. Maybe that's all he found. I don't have anything else."

Farlow looked toward the computer again. "Except the computer, which is still on your desk. And the television." He slid the notebook into his pocket. "Are you insured?"

I smiled, relieved I'd done something right. "Yes. I signed the papers last week."

Officer Farlow raised his eyebrows, pulling out the notebook again. "I see. What value did you place on the vases, for insurance purposes?"

"I didn't, or I don't know. You see, as I said, I inherited the house from my aunt. When I went for insurance, I asked the agent to give me the same coverage she had."

His eyes narrowed. "Hmm. Should itemize if you expect to get reimbursement for this. Do you have photos of the items you say were taken?"

"No. I haven't been here long. Never thought of pictures."

"Ma'am, I'll file your complaint. We'll let you know if we come up with anything. Don't hold your breath." He slapped the notebook shut, put it in his pocket, and took two steps toward the door before turning back to me. "Don't you think it's odd that some old vases were stolen but your computer and television, were left untouched?"

Why is this man so hung up on that old computer and TV?

Frustration oozed out with my answer. "Well, I guess so, but criminals don't always think logically, do they?"

With a slight smile, he stuck his index finger in my

84

face. "That's the truth."

I stepped back and ignored his stare. "And the vases were valuable antiques—at least I think they were." I blew out a breath and averted my eyes. "I was going to have them appraised."

"We'll never know, will we? Unless, of course, we find the perpetrator." Farlow continued to the door. "Good day, ma'am."

After he left, I stood gaping at the closed door, wondering why he'd acted suspicious of me. I hadn't even thought of insurance money. I only wanted to report the break-in.

Chapter Fifteen

My desire for coffee had gone out the door with Officer Farlow, but the can of cocoa in the cupboard looked inviting. An old stand-by comfort food.

I poured milk into a pan, placed it on the stove, and began adjusting the flame when I heard tapping at the screen door.

Wallace Binion stood on the steps. I didn't know him well, but he was a friend of Rarity's.... I hurried to let him in.

Wallace stepped onto the porch and shoved his hands into his pockets. "Sorry to bother you, but I happened to see the squad car in your drive. Did you have some trouble?"

A warm glow pushed its way through my chest and popped into a smile. Someone cared enough to check on me. "It's been a strange morning. I'm making hot chocolate. Why don't you come in and have some with me? I'll tell you all about it."

Wallace laughed. "Hot chocolate. I haven't had that for probably forty years. Sounds great."

I returned to the stove in time to catch the milk before it boiled.

Wallace stood in the middle of the room, shifting his weight from one foot to the other, while I mixed in the cocoa. "This is a nice kitchen. Everything looks the same as when Miss James was here."

I contemplated the script above the window before handing Wallace his mug. Were His mercies new every morning?

"I like it, too."

We sat at the table enjoying hot chocolate while I recounted the events of the morning. "Did you happen to notice anyone in the yard or around the house last night?"

Wallace slowly shook his head. "Shoot. I usually keep an eye on the neighborhood, but I've been out of town a few days. Just got home this morning."

He took a swig of cocoa. "This is good. Reminds me of my youth."

I savored my drink for a minute. "I'm not so upset about the missing vases, as about someone being in my house. It's disconcerting. And Officer Farlow gave the impression he didn't believe me."

Pushing my hair back from my face, I continued. "I guess I can't blame him, I couldn't even describe the vases—just that there were three. I wish I had some kind of proof."

Wallace sat back. "I noticed there were no signs of forced entry in the back. I can take a look at the front, if you like."

"You already checked the back?"

"I did. It's a habit. I notice everything. You can ask Rarity, it makes her crazy, sometimes."

I chuckled. "I think it's a good trait. My friends accuse me of the same thing. Thanks for checking it out. That had to be where they came in. I must have forgotten to bolt it. When I came home, the front door was locked."

"All the same, I'll take a look when I leave. Now about the vases, maybe they're listed on the insurance policy."

"I hope so. The insurance man didn't mention it, but I'll call him first thing tomorrow morning."

We sat in silence, with only the sounds of our sipping and birds whistling outside, breaking the quiet. Beams of sunlight fell across the table. Wallace was a comforting presence—as if I'd known him for years.

I hesitated to disrupt the feeling, but had to ask. "I'm going to ask you something 'off the wall'. Do you know a man named Paul Cooper? He's about my age." He leaned back and set his mug down. "Can't say that I do. Should I?"

"Not really. He was at my class reunion." I discovered my cup was empty and pushed it away. "I have a feeling he isn't who he says he is. Doesn't seem like the person I went to school with. Now, no one else is suspicious, and here I am, popping in after twenty-five years to make accusations. Crazy, huh?"

Wallace shrugged. "I don't know. Sometimes it takes fresh eyes to see what's right in front of you." He leaned to the side and pulled a slip of paper from his pocket. "Do you have a pencil handy? What year did you graduate?"

"Um, '89." I retrieved a pen from my desk and watched Wallace record the year and Paul's name.

He smiled as he stuffed the paper back into his pocket. "I have to write everything down or I forget. I used to run background checks in my business. Now it's kind of a hobby. I'll let you know if I come up with anything."

Wallace stood and deposited his empty cup into the sink. "I better let you get on with your day, and I'm due to pick up Rarity pretty soon. Thank you for the chocolate."

He left through the front door, and studied the area as promised before he cut across the lawn toward his home.

I placed my cup in the sink and went to search out a clean pair of jeans. When the phone rang, I poked my head out of the closet and tossed the jeans on the bed.

Before I could utter a greeting, Clair's voice shrilled. "Lauren, do I ever have news for you."

Not like mine.

"Clair. I'm glad you c—"

"You'll never guess what happened."

Wait, let me tell you.

"Probably not, but listen—"

"There was a shooting in your neighborhood last night."

"What? A shooting? Where? I didn't hear anything."

"It was sort of close to you. Only a few blocks away."

I carried the phone to the living room to peer out at the street. "What shooting? What happened?"

"I got a call from my friend Irma, at the police department. She heard it on her scanner early this morning and went in to find out what was going on. The chief is at the scene right now, at Justice Insurance."

"Justice? Wow, I was there last week. Was anyone hurt?" After pacing once around the living room, I settled into a chair commanding a clear view of the street.

"Hurt? He's dead. Didn't I tell you? One of the agents, Earl Clooney, was killed. You know his wife, Patsy. She works at Rarity's."

"He's Patsy's husband? I never connected them." I paused to suck in air and pointed at the door. "Clair, I just spoke to Earl Clooney yesterday. He was here."

"You're kidding. At your house?" Clair's voice dropped to a whisper. "And now he's dead. Girl, you may have been the last person to see him alive."

"The last person—? Umm. I doubt it. He was here early in the morning."

I stood up to study the street. "Poor Patsy, what will she do? Do they have any idea who did it? Was it a burglary, because I—"

"They don't know anything yet. I wish I could talk longer, but I promised to go to church with Anita. She's been after me for months, and this might be a good time to start. Got to go. I'll let you know if I hear anything." The connection went silent.

Earl Clooney dead? Was it connected with my intruder? I sat down with the phone in my lap. I'd never heard of a homicide in Evelynton. The phone rang again. Startled, I lost my grip and it clattered to the floor.

Retrieving the phone, I found it difficult to voice a greeting.

"Hello, Lauren? It's Rarity. Is that you? Are you all right?"

"Yes, just out of breath." I gulped air.

"Something terrible has happened."

I clenched the receiver. "Oh, I know. I just got off the phone with my friend Clair. She called to tell me about the shooting. It's awful. Have you spoken to Patsy?"

"Yes, for a few minutes and I'm driving over to be with her now."

"How's she taking it?"

"She seemed sort of calm. Probably in shock, poor dear."

I got to my feet and paced to the window. "What can I do to help?"

"Stacy will go into work early in the morning and get on the phone. We're closing the shop tomorrow and will reschedule all Patsy's customers for this week. I told her to take off as long as necessary, so you may have more phoning to do on Tuesday."

Out on the lawn, the cat crouched low to the ground, as Clive Baron stepped out onto his porch. Clive gazed up and down the street, turned, and went back inside.

"Lauren?"

"Hmm? Sorry, I'm here. Of course, I'll even go in tomorrow or Wednesday if you need me."

"It's hard for me to think right now. I imagine the phones will be ringing off the hook with people wanting to know what's going on. Stacy can handle tomorrow, you'll be in on Tuesday, and I'll let you know about Wednesday."

"Okay, call me anytime. I'll have my cell with me."

"You're a God-send. I appreciate it so much. Oh my, Wallace was coming over this morning to take me to church. How could I forget? I'll send him ahead to put Patsy on the prayer chain and then I'll go to her house. Poor girl. She's such a frail thing."

Clicking the phone off, I remained at the window and wondered what happened to peaceful, small town Sundays. In the yard, the cat arched its back and darted under the bush at the corner of the house.

Before I had time to turn away from the window, a squad car skidded to a stop at the curb. I almost clapped as it rolled forward to park in front of my neighbor's blue house, instead of mine.

Officer Farlow must have drawn weekend duty. So glad he'd be talking to my neighbor, not me. I'd had enough of him for one day.

Clive Baron greeted the policeman and they stood conversing on the porch. Clive bent toward the shorter man, in what seemed to be serious conversation. Then they both turned their gaze toward my door. Baron even pointed in my direction. That couldn't be good.

The officer took notes. Pretty soon, he shook Clive's hand and turned to leave.

I waited to watch him climb into his car and drive away, but when he reached the walk, he executed a sharp left turn and directed precise strides to my front porch.

I stood back from the window, out of sight, as he climbed the steps.

I waited. Why did I think he'd change his mind? He knocked. Jimmy Farlow was the last person I wanted to see, but I put on a smile and opened the door.

"Hello, Officer Farlow. Didn't think I'd have the pleasure so soon. What can I do for you?"

"I've had a busy morning, Ms. Halloren. It's been brought to my attention that a Mr. Earl Clooney visited your home early yesterday morning. Is that true?"

"Um. Yes, he was here." This likely from my nosy neighbor. "How did you know?"

"We received a call of suspicious activity, from a concerned citizen."

"Concerned citizen? Since you were next door, I assume that citizen is my neighbor, Mr. Baron. I can't think what you mean by suspicious activity."

"Good citizens report anything they consider relevant when a crime has been committed. What was the purpose of Mr. Clooney's visit so early Saturday morning?"

I let out a drawn-out sigh. I was too tired to feign pleasantness. "He brought an insurance paper for me to sign. I'd been to see him last week, as I think I told you. I guess he'd forgotten to have me sign one form."

"That early? On a Saturday?" I detected a sneer cross Farlow's face. "Very conscientious of him."

"Yes. I guess so. He said he was embarrassed to have missed the page."

"So he made an early morning call? Interesting."

"I wasn't thrilled with the hour either."

Farlow scribbled in his notebook and lifted his eyes to mine. "You see, Ms. Halloren, Mr. Clooney was shot sometime last night. His cleaning lady discovered his body this morning."

"Yes, I know. I got a call from a friend this morning. She wanted me to know, since he was found a few blocks from here."

"A friend? How did she have knowledge of the crime?"

"She knows someone at the police department."

Farlow let out a breath through clenched teeth. "And she knew you were friends with the victim?"

"Not 'friends' with him. I'd only just met him when I got the insurance, and she didn't even know that. She was just worried about me."

"Ms. Halloren, do you own a gun? Any weapons in your house?"

"A gun? No. I hate guns." His attitude grated on my nerves. I couldn't help myself. "I have a steak knife in the kitchen. I guess you might call that a weapon. Does it qualify?" Probably shouldn't be flippant with an officer of the law.

Farlow slapped the notebook closed and stared at me for a few seconds—seemed like five minutes.

"Very funny. Thank you, ma'am." Grim-faced

Officer Farlow tipped his hat and returned to his car.

Chapter Sixteen

Finally dressed for the day, I opened a notebook to list the events of the previous night and organize my thoughts.

Paul Cooper—or whoever he is—wouldn't answer questions, and left the reunion early.

Someone broke into my house.

Someone killed Earl Clooney. Random incidents? Or are they connected?

Am I obsessed with Cooper, as Anita suggested? I should drop it. But what if?

I slapped the notebook shut, tucked it under my arm, and picked up the car keys on the way out of the house.

As Justice Insurance came into view, I applied the brake, slowing the car to a crawl. The street was quiet and the windows of the building dark. But Earl's office was down that long hallway, in the back. A handwritten sign on the front door read, CLOSED. In the lot, a gray sedan sat flanked by two police cars.

Yellow crime scene tape protected the side entrance, as well as the sidewalk leading to the lot. I gawked and allowed my station wagon to inch forward. What was I waiting for? Would they wheel out the body? Most likely it had been removed earlier. Would they drag the murderer out in handcuffs? Not likely. Nothing to see here.

With a sigh, I returned my attention to the road. Unfortunately, I'd drifted left of center and was way too close to an oncoming car. I jerked the wheel to the right and met the eyes of the driver, Paul Cooper, as our vehicles glided past each other. His expression grew hostile, and I turned away.

What's he doing here?

Criminals don't really return to the scene of the crime, do they?

I drove all the way home with my head swiveling from the side mirrors to the rear view and back again. Safely in my driveway, I hurried up the steps and stabbed the door several times before the key entered the lock.

Inside, I leapt onto the sofa, pulled the blanket over my shoulders, then threw it off, and got up to check for activity on the street. Stoneybridge remained quiet.

Several minutes later, my pulse slowed to normal, and my sanity returned, except for talking to myself.

"Why wouldn't Paul scowl at you? You almost crashed into his car."

~

Mundane tasks calm me when nothing else will. Order

makes me feel secure. When Clair called, two hours later, the floors were clean and the laundry done.

"I talked to Irma again. The cleaning lady discovered Earl's body, early this morning. It wasn't suicide and doesn't look like an accident. There's no sign of the weapon."

My knees threatened to give out and I pulled out a dining chair. "Could they tell how long he'd been dead?"

"Irma didn't say, but they interviewed the secretary. She works in the front of the building, and said Earl was still in his office when she left at five. Everyone else had already gone home for the day."

A car with a noisy engine rumbled past the house and I suddenly had goose bumps. "Did they think the shooting had anything to do with the break-ins?"

"Irma didn't say. They caught her eavesdropping and shut the door. She says she's never seen Melvin so shaken. The only people who've died on his watch, have been from old age."

"Yeah. That's kind of what I thought." I walked to the door and double checked the lock.

"Don't you worry." Clair lowered her voice. "I'm sure they have Earl's appointment book, and he probably had other appointments after he saw you. And when they question you, they'll see you couldn't do anything like this."

Question me?

I put my forehead on the door frame. "Oh, thanks Clair. I hadn't considered myself a suspect, until now."

Chapter Seventeen

I couldn't get away from the reception desk and out of The Rare Curl, fast enough. If I had to talk to one more customer, I might bite someone. Women had hovered over me all morning with theories of the murder, ranging from serial killer to alien invasion. I massaged my jaw. It ached from hours of clenched teeth and keeping my opinion to myself.

Outside, I walked resolutely toward my car but stopped at the sight of Anita in Ava's Java. I craved pleasant conversation with my friend.

As soon as the door opened, the familiar aroma of strong coffee, fresh from the grinder, swept over me, relieving tension. I picked up a small cup of Ava's Special Blend and navigated tables to sink into the high-backed chair across from Anita.

"It's good to see you. I need an injection of positive attitude."

She reached over to pat my hand. "I'm sure being in the salon was difficult. How's Patsy?"

I took a sip of coffee and savored the heat in my throat before answering. "I talked to her for a minute on the phone and she seemed unruffled, almost unemotional. She must be stronger than I thought."

"I know. Rarity called the church to say Patsy asked the congregation to discontinue food deliveries." Anita chuckled softly. "I'm sure her refrigerator is overflowing. Our church ladies are enthusiastic givers."

My thoughts flew back to Marc's death. I'd been alone. Would things have been different if we or our friends had been church goers?

Anita blew on her coffee before taking a sip. "She's impressive. Some of the ladies offered to take turns staying with her for a few days but she wanted to be alone and get on with her life."

I set my cup on the table. "She used the words 'get on with my life'? That seems odd."

"That's exactly what she said." Anita nodded. "It seems very soon after Earl's death, but we all deal with grief in different ways."

"Hmm. I guess so. Besides, I know Rarity will be checking in on her."

We sat in silence for a minute and my thoughts wandered to the reunion. "Speaking of getting on. I'm thinking of a new book. The story will be about someone returning to his hometown after a number of years. I'm putting together some research. Do you remember when Paul Cooper came back to Evelynton? Did you recognize him right away?"

Okay, I lied, but I didn't want to be accused of obsession, again.

Anita stared at me through squinty eyes. "For research? Are you sure?"

I produced what I thought to be a believable smile and pulled a notebook from my bag. "I was being silly that night at the reunion. But it spawned the idea for the book. So, how long did it take you to recognize him?"

"Let me think." Anita leaned back and wrapped her hands around her coffee mug. "The first time I saw Paul, he was with Perry. I don't know if I would've known him, because Perry introduced him right away. He walked up and said something like, 'Look who's back, Paul Cooper.'" She puffed her cheeks out and did an amusing imitation of Perry.

"So, you didn't doubt it? You just accepted it?"

Anita tipped her head back and laughed. "Yes, Lauren. I accepted it. I'm very trusting that way. I don't see life as a series of mysteries—like some people I know."

I pressed my hand to my mouth. "Oh. I'm sorry. You're right, I do see mysteries everywhere. But that's what makes a good story."

"And it makes you an entertaining friend."

~

We were still laughing when we left the coffee shop. Anita walked on and I slid behind the wheel of the Chrysler, with every intention of going home. But I soon found myself passing my street and driving toward Paul Cooper's neighborhood.

The scene fascinated me. His perfectly symmetrical house sported pale gray siding, bright white trim, and a white picket fence. Not a blade of grass out of place. With the pots of colorful flowers and professional landscaping, it could have been pulled from a magazine cover.

I slowed to a stop in front of the house, keeping my foot on the brake, and snapped a picture with my phone, before allowing the car to roll on. My rear view mirror reflected a man walking around the corner of the house. It looked like Paul, I couldn't be sure. Without thinking, I punched the accelerator and the tires squealed as the Chrysler lurched forward.

That was smooth.

Once again, I passed my street and motored uptown to Ava's, this time looking for Clair. Had she recognized Paul Cooper when he moved to town? To my delight, Clair occupied her usual table near the window.

Sharp turns aren't easy when driving a monster station wagon, but I managed to cut through traffic and snag a parking place across the street.

Ava gave me a quizzical look. "Welcome back."

I purchased a ham sandwich and carried my plate to join Clair.

Pulling out the same chair I'd sat in earlier. "Glad I caught you—oh, may I join you?"

"Silly question. Of course, sit down. I don't have an appointment for an hour. What's up?" She closed her eyes. "Wait, I don't want to talk about Earl Clooney. That's all anyone wants to talk about. I hope I don't sound shallow, but I can't think about it anymore."

I held up a hand. "Don't worry, it's all I heard at

work today and I'm ready for a break, too."

I bit into my sandwich and took a minute to swallow. "I want to interview you."

Clair brightened. "Interview me? About what?"

"I'm doing a little research to develop the characters for my new novel. These questions may sound strange, but they help me delve into the minds of the players."

Well, I might write a novel about it—someday.

I put the sandwich on the plate and pulled out my notebook. "First question. When did you meet Paul Cooper after he returned to Evelynton? That was about six years ago wasn't it?"

Clair leaned forward on the table and grinned. "Are you still stalking Paul the Impostor?"

Doing my best to appear embarrassed, I forced a small smile. "Oh, no, that was crazy. But as a writer, no experience is wasted. I want to use those fantasies for a character in my book. So could you help me out?"

"Okay girlfriend. It would've been fun if he were a spy, wouldn't it?" Clair leaned back and studied the ceiling. "Anyway, it's probably been six years. Um, I think I met him through Perry. Paul had started working with him at Empire Realty and they came in here, for coffee, one morning."

I tapped my pen on my teeth. "When they walked in, did you recognize him right away? Did you think, 'That man looks familiar.' or 'I've never seen that man in my life.'?"

Clair laughed. "I don't know. I guess I would never have picked him out of a crowd, but when I'm working,

I could walk right past my own mother. I don't know if I even thought about it because Perry introduced him as soon as they walked up."

Angling the notebook so Clair couldn't read it my notation, I scribbled, Perry again.

I tapped the pen on the notebook, still modeling the interested researcher. "Does Paul have relatives in town? Are his parents still around?"

Clair put a well-manicured index finger on her chin. "It seems to me his mother's been gone for ages and his father died a few years ago."

Geesh. Why hadn't I asked this earlier?

"Then his father was alive when Paul moved back to town. Is that true?"

"Sure, he was living at Beaver Creek nursing home. I remember because my aunt June used to go and visit anyone without family. She used to talk about Harry Cooper. He must have been alone until Paul moved home."

I doodled a solid black circle on the notebook page.

Clair's cell phone hummed and vibrated on the table. She pulled it closer to look at the screen. "Sorry, I have to take this."

She stared out the window, lowering her voice, as she spoke to the caller.

A smile lit her face, when she clicked the phone off and tucked it into her bag. Stuffing papers into her briefcase, she said, "I have to go. The Muhollands are writing an offer. Hurray!"

In one fluid movement, she picked up her handbag

and briefcase while scooting her chair out. "Good to see you. Anita and I are meeting here Thursday morning. Join us?"

She was halfway to the door when I answered. She stepped out onto the sidewalk as I wrote in my notebook. Both parents deceased. Check out Beaver Creek Nursing Home—Harry Cooper.

That visit just might settle the matter, but it would wait until tomorrow.

I was anxious to be home, so I gobbled my sandwich without tasting it. If I was totally wrong about Paul, who killed the insurance man?

~

Rarity's familiar smile shown through the little window in the door. Who else would be knocking at six in the morning? I released the bolt and pulled the door open.

"Good morning Rarity. This is a surprise."

"Good morning. I'm so glad you're up. Have you been out to see the sunrise?

I shook my head.

"You must see it. Step out and admire God's glory. It's absolutely gorgeous."

The porch chilled my bare feet, but the fresh morning air made me wonder why I didn't get up early more often. Glowing shades of pink, peach, and apricot filled the sky with beams emanating from the rising sun. Not a bad way to begin the day.

"How about some coffee? I haven't had any yet."

"Oh dear, almost forgot what I came for. Not just to admire the sunrise. I wanted to see if you would deliver a casserole to Patsy for me. At a decent hour, of course. It's way too early now. I'm on my way to work and won't have any time to take it until late this afternoon.

Assuming my consent, she retreated down the steps.

"Just a moment, I'll get it from the car. Wanted to make sure you were up." She trotted to her car and pulled out the dish, wrapped in a towel.

Climbing back up onto the porch, she handed it to me. It was heavy and hot.

"I know Patsy said she didn't need any more food but this is really nutritious. Anyway, I think someone should stop in every day to check on her, and this provides as good an excuse as any. I'm sure she's seen enough of me already. You don't mind taking it, do you?"

"It's no trouble. I'm happy to take it."

Even through the towel, the heat began to burn my fingers, and I looked for a place to set it down.

"You cooked this casserole already this morning? While you got ready for work?"

"Sure. It's easy to whip up, and I got dressed while it baked."

"You'll probably be safe stopping by any time after ten. I'm not telling her you're on the way because I want you to see how she's doing. Don't want her to have time to put on an act. You'll get a feel for it by the way she looks. You know—if she's pale, or looks tired as if she hasn't slept. Just talk to her and ascertain her state of mind."

I wondered what we would talk about. We worked

together and still had only one short conversation, previously.

Rarity continued. "Patsy always insists everything is fine, but you know how some people would say they're okay, no matter what. Tell her this is her favorite dish. It's chicken and vegetables. I know she likes it. Easy to warm up, so she'll have something good to eat."

~

At ten o'clock, I loaded the food into the passenger side of the Chrysler, wishing I'd thought of an excuse not to go. What would I say? I'd rather avoid contact with the bereaved. Maybe, my past experience should have prepared me to comfort another woman in pain, instead of driving me away.

I argued with myself on my way. Anita. I should have called Anita. She'd be here in a flash.

I talked to myself in the mirror. "Grow up Lauren. This is what grown-up people do—comfort others."

I needn't have worried about coming face to face with a grief-stricken woman. Patsy opened the door, beaming. As recognition dawned, her expression morphed to neutral—noncommittal. Was she expecting someone?

I must quit being suspicious. She might have been indulging in some happy memories, thinking of better days, and my unexpected appearance brought her back to reality.

"Hi, Patsy. How are you today? I've been thinking of you, and wanted to check in." I held up the cooled casserole dish. "This delicious treat is straight from

Rarity's kitchen."

She stared at me.

"I know you must have tons of food, but you know Rarity, afraid you might not be eating. She had to send one more thing to tempt you. It's your favorite—chicken."

Her awkward silence hung between us.

"Have I come at a bad time? I won't stay long, just checking if there's anything I can do for you today."
I wondered if she had taken a tranquilizer. If I'd ever seen an expressionless face, this was it.

After a few agonizing, silent, seconds, Patsy's voice came out clear and strong. "No, there's nothing I need. But how kind of you to ask. I'm really getting along so well. And thank you for bringing the casserole. I love Rarity's casseroles. She's a wonderful cook."

What would Anita do in this situation? I began to edge inside, slid one foot forward, then the other. That's as far as I got, Patsy stood her ground. I thought about how I'd shut myself away after Marc's death.

But Patsy showed no signs of the desperation and sorrow I remembered. Her hair was combed. She wore full makeup, eyeliner not even smudged.

I glanced over her shoulder. The living room was cluttered. A fresh box of tissues balanced on the arm of a chair. Magazines and paperbacks littered the sofa and coffee table.

Flowers. A bright pot of them occupied the middle of the table. Very colorful, but in need of water. A few wilted blooms hung over the side of the pot.

"There must be something I can help you with.

Have you been to the funeral home to make arrangements?"

"No. I'll just go to Klinc Funeral Parlor and have him incinerated."

"Cremated?"

"Yeah. That's it. I have to wait until they release Earl's body, anyway. I'm not worried about it."

"Call me if you want someone to go with you."

Patsy raised her voice. "I'll be sure to call if I need anything. Thank you for coming, and thank Rarity for sending the food. I know it will be delicious." She chuckled. "Gosh, there's so much, I'm going to get fat. Bye now."

I took the hint and stepped back across the threshold. Patsy bumped the door with her hip, and it swung closed.

I sat in the Chrysler for a moment before starting the engine, thinking she was very strong, or very much in denial. Maybe she hadn't taken the time to think about how her life would change.

Chapter Eighteen

"Thanks so much for coming in on your day off. I must've been crazy to think we could handle it. Phone's ringing constantly with women wanting information." Rarity gave my shoulder a squeeze and hustled back to her styling chair.

"Not a problem, Rarity. I wasn't accomplishing anything at home anyway. I couldn't concentrate." I took my place at the desk and fielded calls for an hour until the phones went silent, and I welcomed a chance to breathe.

Chills ran up my spine as I felt the warmth of a presence close to my back. Glancing up, I was relieved to see Stacy leaning over my shoulder. She pointed at the appointment book and whispered. "Gladys Murphy is coming in. There, in Rarity's column. Gladys is the cleaning lady at Justice Insurance. She's the one who found the body."

"No kidding? This will be interesting." My thoughts

raced, wondering what the crime scene would have looked like. Was the place ransacked? What evidence would have been there?

Thirty minutes later, right on time for her appointment, Gladys Murphy pushed the door open. Her light blue sweat pants and mauve ruffled blouse were clean and pressed, but her short brown hair had a serious case of bed-head. As soon as she stepped inside, her gaze darted to Rarity's chair. The woman's face softened with relief when Rarity walked up to meet her.

"Gladys, it's so good to see you. How are you?" Rarity put an arm around the woman's shoulders and escorted her to the styling station. Safely settled in the chair, Gladys started blabbing as if she'd spent days waiting for someone to listen.

"I was just doing my job, same as always. Earl wanted me to clean on Sundays, but I like to have family time on the Lord's day, so I went in real early. Earl's office was always my worst job. The man's too cheap to pay for cleaning more than once every other week." Her eyes opened wide, and she peered up at Rarity, "Oh, forgive me. I didn't mean to speak ill of the dead."

Rarity kept her voice soothing and leaned close to the woman. "Don't worry, Gladys. I know this has been a terrible strain on you. You can tell me anything you want. No judgment here."

I hurried to the break room, poured a cup of coffee, and brought it back to offer to Gladys. She smiled and cradled the warm mug with both hands before setting it down. I slid into a chair close by, waiting for her to continue.

"Had my arms full of cleaning supplies and I was pulling the vacuum sweeper in. Walking backwards so I could push the door open with my backside. All of a sudden, I tripped over something and thought, 'Crap, what's he left on the floor now?' Turned out to be Earl's foot." She shook her head and waved a hand. "Well, I fell right down, and the window cleaner and sponges went flying. I ended up sprawled out on the floor, and when I came to my senses, I looked over and there was Earl's face."

Gladys grabbed Rarity's arm. "He was right next to me, staring at something over my shoulder. I swear, I almost turned to see what he was looking at, but then it came to me. He wasn't looking at anything. He was dead. Dead!"

Gladys covered her eyes for a minute, then dropped her hands to her lap while Rarity patted her shoulder.

After a deep breath, Gladys continued. "There was blood all over the front of his white shirt. I tell you, I scrambled to my feet as fast as I could, and ran over behind the desk. I wasn't thinking, 'cause when I got there, I wished I'd headed the other way, to the door. I wanted to get out of there, but had to stay 'cause Earl was between me and the way out."

Rarity nodded knowingly. "How awful for you."

Gladys seemed to be talked out. Rarity just stood there and held her hand. I couldn't stand the quiet. "What did you do then?"

This brought the woman back to the subject. "It took me a while to get my wits about me, but there was a phone right there on the desk, so I called 911. Then, I sat down on the floor, in the corner, and I prayed the Lord's Prayer until the police came."

She looked into the mirror for the first time, grabbed one of Rarity's brushes, and passed it through her hair.

"They came in and said it was all right and I should get up, but I told them, 'No way.' I was going to stay right where I was 'til they took Earl's body away." She threw the brush down and it went skidding off the table.

While recovering the brush from the floor, Rarity asked, "Did they take him away?"

"Well, no. Melvin said I'd be more comfortable in one of the other offices. He's such a nice man. He put his arm around me, put his hand over my eyes, and led me out to the hallway." Gladys relaxed and sat back in her chair.

I couldn't stop myself. "Could you tell what happened? While you were waiting for the police, did you notice anything about the office? Something out of the ordinary?"

Gladys' mouth flew open and her head swiveled toward me. "Something out of the ordinary? You mean, other than Earl's dead body and the puddle of blood on the carpet? No ma'am, I didn't see anything else and I didn't want to see anything else." With that, she turned back to Rarity. It reminded me of a child looking to her mother.

Rarity patted Gladys' shoulder. "Let's get your hair done. You just relax and let me take care of everything."

I retreated to my desk, wondering how to find out if Earl handled Paul Cooper's insurance.

Chapter Nineteen

The mailbox produced a fresh set of bills, forcing fanciful dreams of authoring a true crime novel from my head. I dedicated the remainder of the day to gainful employment, polishing and submitting a magazine article.

Later, in the dark, images of Paul Cooper flitted through my mind's eye. I tossed and turned in bed, wondering why everyone took his identity for granted. In the early hours of the morning, with crickets singing outside, my exhausted brain surrendered to sleep.

However, upon opening my eyes to sunlight, the mantra returned. Why believe him? Clair and Anita met Paul through Perry. When did Perry meet Paul?

I planned my interview with Perry while shampooing my hair. By the time I stepped out of the shower, I was in full interview mode, so I passed the blow dryer through my hair and grabbed some clothes. The business card, he'd handed me at the reunion, lay at the bottom of my handbag. It listed his office address and I decided to take a chance on him being there.

Thirty minutes later, I almost missed the sign for Empire Realty. The office building could best be described as a rambling, country home. I approached the structure with a sense of awe. It may have been the only building in Evelynton with an entrance framed with Crown molding and white pillars. As I tentatively opened the ornate door, I half expected to be welcomed by the butler. Instead, a quirky tune of door chimes sounded my entrance.

The room oozed luxury. Within seconds, a tall, slender woman strode into view from a side entrance. Her flowing dress and sleek French twist gave her an air of lady of the manor.

I stood gaping while she extended her hand. "Hello, welcome to Empire Realty. I'm Judith. May I help you?"

I shut my mouth and returned the handshake. In my jeans, I felt as if I'd wandered out of Evelynton, into another dimension. "Hi, um hello. I'm Lauren Halloren. I'd like to see Perry Sizemore. I'm sorry, I don't have an appointment but hoped he might have a few minutes."

Her reply rolled out as smooth as silk, "Of course. Won't you have a seat." She directed me to a royal blue sofa. "I'll see if Mr. Sizemore is free, Ms. Halloren. May I offer you a cup of coffee or a soft drink, while you wait?"

"Thank you, no, I'm fine." I sank into the velvet cushions and Judith soundlessly slipped from the room, her footsteps muffled by deep pile carpeting.

I'd begun sorting through home decorating magazines when Perry burst into the room. His impressive mass propelled toward me, and I froze, fearful of being smothered in a massive bear hug. But he skidded to a stop and grabbed my hands.

"Hey beautiful, it's so good to see you. I'm glad you stopped in." Releasing one hand, he gestured toward the door from which he'd been ejected. "We'll talk in my office."

The door opened into a short hallway. We entered a drab little office. The room was maybe ten by ten, with a desk and bookshelves constructed of fake wood. Perry pulled out one of two stained, upholstered chairs for me, and with some difficulty, squeezed behind the desk. A rush of air escaped the cushion as he settled into the massive vinyl chair. Perry leaned back and tented his fingers in front of his chest. "How is everything, Lauren? If it's possible, you are even more gorgeous now than you were in high school." He lowered his voice to a confidential tone. "You know, I always had a crush on you."

Eew.

I sat, speechless. What was I supposed to say to that? The twinkle in his eye made me nervous.

After a slight pause, where he gazed past me with glassy eyes, Perry raised his voice to sales pitch level. "So, are you thinking of selling the Cape Cod? Interested in a new home?" He gave a quick nod and a wink. "Something more up to date? I have two outstanding listings that are just your style. Ultra-modern, open concept, country setting. Lots of room for entertaining."

My style?

I shook my head and tried to smile. "I'm sure they're beautiful, but I'm here on a different mission. I'm constructing a story line for a book, and I knew you could be of help. It's a mystery. The idea came to me at our class reunion."

Perry leaned forward and rested his elbows on the desk. His eyes got big and his voice came out in a secretive hiss. "Ah, a mystery. Of course Lauren. This is exciting. What's it about?"

"I can't tell you much. That goes against a rule I have—never let anyone in on the plot until it's well underway."

Perry maintained his conspiratorial tone. "I understand. What's your question for me? Shoot."

I leaned forward and smiled. "I can tell you this much. One of the characters moves back to her hometown after many years, and no one remembers her. Of course, I have lots of experience from my own return, but what would I do if no one knew me? For instance, I know Paul Cooper lived out of state for quite a while, and moved back several years ago. What do you remember about his return?"

Perry looked up at the ceiling and scratched his second chin. "As I remember it, that would have been five or six years ago."

My pen poised above the notebook, ready to record his revelations. "Uh-huh, how did you first run into him? Did he come to see you? Did someone introduce you?"

Perry aimed a blank stare at me. "I don't know." He pointed a chubby index finger toward the ceiling. "Wait. I saw his name on a roster of homes sold. Took notice because the house was on my street. I like to know my neighbors. Well, I saw the name and thought 'Old Paul's back in town.' As soon as he'd moved in, I went down to see him. Turned out, I was the first of the old gang."

I made a note. "Really? That's a coincidence—Paul moving into your neighborhood. I'll bet he was glad to see you. What did he say? Did he recognize you right away?" I leaned back and directed my pen toward Perry. "I don't think you've changed at all since high school."

Perry sat up straighter and his smile widened. "You know, I try to keep in shape. Play a lot of golf." After a pause, he continued. "No, I think Paul was kind of puzzled at first and shocked to see me standing on his doorstep." Perry slapped the desk. "Then, I identified myself. Let him off the hook, you know. After all, it had been over fifteen years."

I nodded, smiling. "That's a long time. How about Paul, did you think he had changed at all?"

Perry rotated his chair to the side and made two attempts to cross his legs before giving up. "He'd aged, for sure, but I have an eye for faces, and a strong memory."

"That's a gift, Perry. I'm afraid my memory isn't that good."

Perry laced his fingers across his ample stomach. "It's important in my business. I work at it. As luck would have it, Paul's in real estate, so I got him a position right here at Empire."

Here?

"He has an office here?" I blew out a slow breath in an effort to maintain a calm facade.

"He does, even though he rarely uses it. He works from home most days. I see him more on the golf course than in the office." Perry's chair squeaked as he pivoted it toward me again. "Say, your book isn't about Paul, is it? He's a private kind of guy. Got a little peeved at me when I introduced him around. 'Course I told him, in real estate, you have to know people."

I waved a hand in Perry's direction. "No. The book isn't about Paul. I'm only building characters right now. I thought of Paul because of his experience, wondering if it was the same as mine. Everyone seems to know me."

"Hey. How could anyone miss you? You look the same, only more alluring." He winked at me.

Eek.

"Have you talked to Paul yet? I could set it up for you. He's a loner, but I'm closer to him than anyone— except Missy of course." He chuckled.

I glanced at the closed door. "He isn't here today, is he?"

"Oh, no. Probably at home, but just say the word and I'll call him. Or maybe I could drive you over to his house, in my Caddy."

I retrieved my handbag from the floor. "Thanks, Perry, but I don't think I'll need to bother him at this time. I doubt it'll be necessary at all. I have a lot of information already."

"Okay, but I'd be happy to call him and pave the way for you. Maybe we could all meet for drinks?"

"That's very kind of you, but don't bother Paul. I'm sure I have all I need." I tucked my notebook into my handbag and pulled the strap over my shoulder.

"It's been great talking to you Perry. You've been so much help." I put out my hand before I thought about it. "I won't keep you any longer. I know you have work to do."

Perry stood up, quickly pushed himself around the desk, and captured my hand in both of his. "It's been great talking to you, Lauren. Stop by anytime. We'll have lunch." Maintaining a one-handed grip on me, he pulled a business card from his pocket. "Take my card. It has both my private office and cell number on it. His eyes bored into mine.

Carefully extracting my hand. "Oh, I have your card, Perry. Thanks so much." I pulled open the office door and made a hasty exit down the hall and through the sitting room, hearing the chimes as I escaped to the parking lot.

While I turned the ignition, the conversation replayed in my mind. Perry said he'd recognized Paul, but did he really? Was it simply because of the name and expectations? Would Perry admit to being wrong about anything? I had yet to find anyone who changed my suspicions about Paul's identity.

At the first intersection, I pulled to the curb and slammed on the brakes.

Chapter Twenty

pulled out my notebook and flipped back two pages. The names Harry Cooper and Beaver Creek Nursing flashed at me like a neon sign.

Oh crap.

I'd forgotten to check out that lead. Or maybe, since it didn't fit into my scenario, I'd intentionally pushed it aside.

No time like the present to make that visit.

~

Acrid fumes of antiseptic assaulted my nose and stung my eyes in the Beaver Creek foyer. The wheelchair-bound residents, clustered inside, seemed unaffected by the smell. I smiled and answered the chorus of greetings, murmuring "hello" to each as I wove through the wheels. With a slight wave to the elderly group, I headed toward a reception desk at the end of a short hall.

I waited to speak until the young aid looked up from her magazine. She must have been engrossed in the article, for she seemed surprised to see me.

"Hi. I have a question about a former resident. I wonder if you remember Harry Cooper." She directed a blank stare at me and I was about to repeat myself when a tall, slim woman stepped to the desk, clipboard in hand. Her badge read Helen Peters—Activities Director.

I began again. "Hi, I'm Lauren Halloren. I—."

Her face lit up with a ready smile. "I know that name—Ruth James' niece, Lauren Grace. I heard you inherited. Ruth was a wonderful woman. She was here quite often, reading stories to the residents, and planning birthday parties."

"Really? My aunt volunteered here?" I still struggled to digest the idea of this new Aunt Ruth.

Helen put her hand on my arm and leaned in. I breathed in her flowery cologne, a welcome deliverance from the antiseptic cloud. "Oh my, such a loss. The residents loved her—we all did. She is missed." She slowly shook her head.

Speechless, my mouth hung open for a moment. "I had no idea."

"She was a jewel. We'll never find another volunteer like her."

Helen pulled the clipboard to her chest. "What can I do for you?"

"I'm a freelance writer doing a newspaper story about forgotten nursing home residents. I want to bring to light the plight of living out their last years without visitors." Lying again, but I think I sounded sincere. So I will do the story, sometime. "I've been doing research, and a friend mentioned a man named Harry Cooper."

Helen's eyes twinkled. "Oh, I remember Harry. Sweet man. He didn't say much, but always had a smile on his face." She paused. "But he did have family. His son visited every week toward the end."

"He did visit?"

You see, the son had lived out of state for a long time, then moved back, and was very attentive until Harry passed away."

"Oh, that's nice, Harry got to be with him before he died." I nodded, and mentally shredded my notes.

"Yes. The son—I wish I could remember his name. Anyway, he didn't think Harry knew him, but I like to think somewhere in his heart, Harry knew his boy had come home. He—."

I put up my hand. "I'm sorry, I don't understand. Oh wait, did Harry have Alzheimer's?"

"No. It was vascular dementia from years of high blood pressure, not that it matters much to family. They just feel forgotten. Harry didn't outwardly recognize anyone, but I'm quite sure he was with us in spirit. Such a shame his son didn't make it home while Harry was lucid. They could have had some nice talks. Harry passed a few months after their reunion."

Helen chuckled and tapped herself on the head. "But about your story, I'll introduce you to some other residents. How wonderful, to have a story in the paper, letting people know that even Alzheimer and dementia patients love visitors. Come with me."

Helen put her arm around my shoulders and

guided me into the first hall. "Louise is in the first room. We'll start with her."

The intercom squawked nearby and caused me to levitate a few inches. Helen merely raised her eyebrows. "Wouldn't you know it? I'm needed. You go right in." She began backing away, clutching her clipboard to her chest. "I'll check back with you soon. If I get tied up, check please come in anytime. There are more residents who would make perfect subjects. I can't wait to tell the director about your story."

Helen took a few steps backward down the hall. "Check at the desk. Debbie will give you my hours." She then turned on her heel and speed-walked toward her destination, blond hair flying in the breeze.

I glanced in the direction of the receptionist. She eyed me with interest, so I smiled and opened the door to Louise's room.

How could I escape?

A diminutive woman sat in an upholstered chair. Her tiny feet, in orthopedic shoes, dangled an inch or so above the floor. A halo of white fuzz surrounded a face composed of softly folded skin, that appeared almost transparent. On her television, women jumped up and down in front of a game board, while bells rang, and music played. The noise was enough to drive me bonkers, but Louise sat peacefully with her head tilted to one side.

I raised my voice above the ruckus. "Hello, Louise. My name is Lauren. May I talk to you for a few minutes?" No response. I'd leaned over to repeat the question when I noticed her closed eyelids. I stood still and watched her chest until it raised and lowered, confirming she was breathing. I tip-toed out.

The receptionist's attention was now buried in her magazine.

I slipped out the front door and walked away clenching my fist. "What have I gotten myself into now? Writing a story about a nursing home? I'll have to stop by the newspaper office, talk to the editor, sell him on the idea. They probably don't pay much, if anything."

A man studied me as I passed. Talking to myself. Probably thinks I'm an escapee.

I wrote in my notebook. 'Harry Cooper—not a reliable witness to the identity of his son.' Then again, that didn't prove Paul wasn't who he claimed. It might be just as Helen said. He'd waited too long to come home.

Chapter Twenty-one

It was a typical Saturday morning at The Rare Curl as I walked in and took my place at the reception desk—every chair already filled with a woman anticipating her new hairstyle.

Every chair? Patsy's workplace captured my attention. Although I didn't see Patsy, her chair held a customer, complete with shampoo cape and cup of coffee. A brief scan of the appointment book confirmed Patsy had indeed returned to work.

Rarity scurried from the break-room and joined me.

"Patsy's back to work already?" After Marc died. I'd stayed in seclusion for months, which in retrospect wasn't a healthy way to cope.

Rarity ran her finger down the column of her appointments. "Yes, poor thing. She's so brave. Just wants to move on with her life, and I know she needs the income, at least until Earl's life insurance pays."

"Yeah. The bills don't quit coming in just because

you're in mourning."

"Right now, Patsy's in the break-room, speaking to a police officer about Earl's death."

Forgetting where we were, I spun around to face Rarity. "They're questioning Patsy? Why don't they leave her alone? Can't a woman grieve in peace?"

I sputtered. "Patsy has enough to deal with, without having to repeatedly talk with the police. They can't think sweet Patsy's involved." I took a breath and shifted my gaze around the shop. The room had grown deadly quiet. Chatter had ceased and every eye focused on me.

Rarity put her hand on my shoulder and whispered, "Oh, they're probably asking if Earl had any enemies or if he'd had any run-ins with anyone. I'm sure they're just doing their job."

Why must she always be so calm?

Still sputtering, but quietly. "I'm afraid I'm not as understanding as you are. It's unthinkable to put a woman through that. She has to live with the knowledge of her husband's murder and then defend herself against stupid questions and accusations. After they questioned me about Marc's death, I was a mess for weeks."

"Oh dear, how could I forget?" Rarity whispered. "You have firsthand experience. This must bring back a lot of pain. Don't worry, I don't think the investigator will be hard on Patsy. I spoke to him earlier and he seems like a nice man."

We turned at the familiar squeak of the break-room door. Patsy emerged, dabbing her eyes with a tissue. She put on a smile and walked straight to her customer.

Sure, I just bet he's a nice man.

My mouth dropped open when the door squeaked again. It was Mr. Beautiful from the Java Shop, Mr. Tall Dark Stranger from my first day in Evelynton. Not as appealing now, he appeared more sinister than I'd noticed before. I turned and picked up my pencil, busying myself with studying appointments, as I heard his footsteps approach.

Rarity chirped an introduction. "Lauren Halloren, this is Agent Spencer. He's with the FBI." She made him sound like a visiting celebrity.

I raised my chin, keeping my expression noncommittal. "FBI? In this small town?"

He smiled down at me and I squeezed my lips together, fighting the urge to smile in return. "Yes, ma'am. I'm in town on an unrelated matter—visiting a friend." His deep voice made me want to sigh, but I warned myself not to be fooled. "Officer Farlow is ill, so I offered my assistance for a few days. I see in my notes, you've been interviewed."

"So kind of you to help out. Yes, I spoke to Officer Farlow. Told him everything I know—which is nothing." I congratulated myself on maintaining a professional tone, although, in retrospect, it may have sounded sharp.

Agent Spencer blinked. "I won't take up any more of your time. Unless you've thought of something since that interview?"

His warm, soothing, voice threatened to

undermine my resolve. With effort, I kept my countenance stern. "No, I don't have anything else to say." I turned my eyes to the appointment book. "So, you don't have to waste your time on me."

Out of the corner of my eye, I saw him straighten and slide his notebook into his pocket.

To Rarity, he said, in that penetrating voice, "Thank you for your cooperation, ma'am. I'll let you know if we need any more information."

I could hear the smile in Rarity's words. "Thank you, Agent Spencer. Just let me know if I can do anything. I hope you find the person who did this."

I looked up briefly when he said, "Thank you, Ms. Halloren." With a sideways glance and a nod, Mr. FBI left the salon.

Rarity returned to her styling chair while I took several deep breaths.

Later, on my way to the coffee pot, I passed Patsy, deep in conversation with her customer. "You know Earl. He liked to have fun. He often stayed out until the wee hours. It was Sunday morning before I even noticed he wasn't home."

Chapter Twenty-two

Visions of Patsy's interrogation played in my head until my shift ended. No, I wasn't in the room, but I could imagine.

Still muttering about invasive police procedure, I slid over the hot vinyl upholstery of my car. I rolled down the windows and pulled into traffic, to drive the familiar route toward home.

My heart ached for Patsy, suddenly alone. The thought of her husband's murder made my head spin. Who could've killed Earl? And why? He was a simple, small town, insurance agent—with a phobia for caffeine. Yet someone brought a gun to his office and shot him. That meant premeditation—not a crime of passion, didn't it? A thief? Random gang initiation?

There aren't any gangs in Evelynton.

Whoever it was, would that person kill again?

Lost in my thoughts, I didn't notice I'd rolled past the stop sign until the car horn blared. Tires squealed and a car swerved around me. I screamed and slammed on my brakes, noticing the other car for the first time. The driver, Paul Cooper, glared straight at me. His lips formed a tight, straight line. He whipped his attention back to the road ahead and sped away.

My heart pounded in free-form rhythm as I watched his car disappear down the street. Eventually, with big gulps of air, my breathing slowed.

After looking both ways, I continued through the intersection. Trading my resolve for auto safety for the safety of home, I pressed harder on the accelerator, and picked up speed as I got closer. By the time I skidded to a stop in the driveway, my fingers cramped from gripping the steering wheel.

Maybe it was the scare at the intersection or the hate in Paul's face. Something brought back a memory locked away for years. I climbed out of the car, thrust open the front door, and ran to the closet under the stairs. Crawling on hands and knees, I reached to the back, found the box, and tugged it into the light.

Five-year-old packing tape crackled as I tore it off. Wedged into the bottom of the box, under wads of crumpled newspaper, was the item that had leapt to mind at the sight of the devil in Paul Cooper's eyes.

I opened a black, hard-plastic container holding the handgun Marc had shocked me with long ago.

I could still hear his voice. "I know this will surprise you, but I keep a gun with me when I work. It's for protection, and I want you to be safe, too."

Surprised? Make that stunned. "I hate guns. Why do I need one? And why do you? You're a photographer."

"Photojournalist." He corrected me.

Then he'd gripped my shoulders and gazed into my eyes. "Lauren, I want you to be able to defend yourself. The world isn't as safe as you think. I keep mine in the glove compartment and I want you to take this with you when you go out." He'd insisted on teaching me to use it, and dragged me to the shooting range for practice.

Not long after that conversation, I'd discovered the wisdom of his words. The world wasn't safe. Only, the gun hadn't helped my husband. He never had the chance to defend himself against the stray bullet that took his life.

Memories of my training flooded back. Marc's hands loading the gun, unloading, and his insistence that I repeat the process. I remembered everything, performed each step, and slipped the cold black weapon into my handbag.

I'd be smarter from now on. No more questions about Paul Cooper. Why had I been so naive, believing I could get information without his knowledge? No one ever called me a good liar. Had I forgotten how small this town was? About the gossip? There must be other ways to obtain information.

I sat at my computer and spent the next few hours scrolling through Internet databases. Finally, I rested my elbows on the desk and my face in my hands.

Pages of the obviously wrong Paul Cooper—too old, too young. The little information pertaining to the man I looked for, was not nearly enough. Paul had been married after college but divorced six months later. I would've liked to talk to his ex-wife, but after the divorce decree, she disappeared from the search results.

Similarly, Paul had done nothing Internet worthy until he obtained his real estate license, a year before returning to Evelynton.

I found the license for his marriage to Missy. Very little information for twenty-five years. What use would it be?

Chapter Twenty-Three

I approached the door with caution, leery of answering the knock, even in daylight hours. Like everyone else in town, I wouldn't open my door to just anyone. Evelynton had been eerily quiet in the two weeks since the murder. Less laughter at Ava's. Fewer neighborly visits.

I peeked through the window. Anita peered back at me, bouncing on her toes. Clair hovered close behind.

As soon as the door opened, they crowded in and began talking simultaneously, then eyed each other. Clair opened her hand toward Anita, giving her the floor.

"Lauren, we were so glad to see your car in the drive. Couldn't wait to tell you. They've made an arrest in Earl's murder, but you won't guess who it is."

Clair headed for the kitchen. "I need a glass of water. Anyone else want one?"

Keeping my eyes on Anita, I shook my head.

Anita plopped down on the sofa. "You won't believe it.

Yes, I will. They got him.

Allowing myself a smug smile, I sat next to Anita and waited to hear my suspicions confirmed. "Tell me."

"A nurse, of all people. Her name's Helen Peters, and she works at Beaver Creek Nursing Home."

Wait, who?

I tucked my feet up underneath me and turned to face Anita. "You're kidding. Helen Peters? I met her a few of weeks ago, when I went to the nursing home, um, to research a story."

Clair rushed back into the room. "The labs came back yesterday. Remember my informant, Irma, at the police department? She called me this morning to report she overheard they'd matched Helen's fingerprints to a coffee cup found at the crime scene. And they're pretty sure her hair matches the strands found on the body."

I shook my head and looked up at Clair. "That can't be right. Why would they have Helen's fingerprints? Does she have a record?"

"Complete stroke of luck." Anita answered, drawing my attention back to her. "Remember the break-in at the nursing home last year?"

Clair shrieked and I flashed a glance at her. "Oh no, you wouldn't. Before you moved back."

Anita took over again. "Anyway, there was a robbery, and they fingerprinted all the employees in order to isolate the prints that didn't belong. It was a big deal because drugs were involved."

She shrugged and raised her hands in the air. "Turns out they didn't need the prints because they caught a resident's grandson selling prescription drugs. Not a very smart kid. The labels, with patient names, were still on the bottles."

Clair took over and my gaze snapped back to her. "So, lo and behold, when they ran the prints from the coffee cup, up pops Helen. It was all top-secret, and Irma couldn't say anything until today, when they made the arrest."

"Melvin and Jimmy Farlow walked right into the nursing home and marched her out in handcuffs." That was Anita.

I felt like a ping-pong ball.

I rubbed my neck, dizzy from the volley. "I only spoke to her a few minutes, but Helen seemed like a kind person. I wouldn't have guessed she could hurt a flea. And who would think she'd own a gun? Did they find the gun?"

"Not yet." Clair finished her water and hovered over us. "But I'm sure it's only a matter of time. She probably disposed of it, maybe threw it in the lake." She demonstrated with the glass, thankfully not releasing it.

Clair pointed the glass, splattering me with a few drops of water. "It's always the quiet ones. The ones you don't suspect." She paused for a breath and I rescued the glass, depositing it on the coffee table. "Don't we always see on the news that someone's nice quiet neighbor has bodies buried in the backyard?"

Anita and I were mute. That's true. It's always the ones you don't suspect.

Clair broke the silence. "Gosh, I lost track of time. Anita, I have to drop you off and get back to work."

"Lauren, I'm meeting Irma tonight at Burgers and Bean Sprouts. She's going to fill me in on the story. Why don't you meet us?"

"Absolutely. Where is this place?"

"It's a new place on Route 27. Just drive north and you'll see it. It's a few miles, but Irma doesn't want to be seen by anyone from work. Five o'clock. Want to come, Anita?"

Anita shook her head. "I'll be cooking dinner. You can tell me about it later."

After seeing them out, I crossed my arms over my chest and leaned against the door. I may have to rethink my goal of writing true crime. Obviously, I'm not a reliable judge of character. What if my niche is travelogues and informational articles, read only by senior citizens?

~

I found Burgers and Bean Sprouts at five minutes after five. Four cars parked around what seemed to be a converted 1960's gas station, sans gas pumps. Once inside, the atmosphere became warm and inviting. Booths, with deep red upholstery, lined the perimeter, and eight or ten tables filled the center of the room. A mouth-watering aroma of hamburgers and sauteed onions drifted in from the kitchen. A waitress approached me and I pointed to the ladies at the only occupied booth.

I made my way to the far side of the room and Clair introduced me to the tiny woman sitting across from her. Irma reached up to shake my hand. Hers was childlike in size, bony, with soft, loose skin. I would have guessed her to be sixty or sixty-five if her eyes weren't so bright.

The dialog seemed to have been in progress, but they made no attempt to bring me up to speed. I slid into the booth beside Clair, and Irma launched into a continuation of her story.

"Melvin worked so hard on this case—came in early and worked late. He was fit to be tied. Kept trudging from one office to the next, dragging Jimmy Farlow with him, carrying stacks of papers. Then half the papers would land in the trash." Irma paused to sip her Coke while the waitress dropped off a basket of curly fries and asked me for my order.

I declined. Irma squirmed until the waitress left the table. Her face was so animated I revised my guess as to her age. Forty?

Her fingers worked vigorously rolling her straw wrapper into a little ball as she continued. "Melvin was making himself crazy, talking to himself all day long. Nothing I could make out—just muttering. But then the information about the fingerprints came in, and boy did his mood change. The way he strutted around, you'd have thought he'd been elected mayor."

I rested my elbows on the table, leaning closer. "That's all the evidence he has? Just the fingerprints?"

"That's all he needs. They don't have the forensics back on the hair, but it's blond, just like Helen's.

Melvin went right over to Beaver Creek, took Farlow with him, and brought Helen Peters back in handcuffs." Irma beamed.

"Melvin solved his first murder. That'll make the paper, maybe even the nationals." This was Clair.

Irma snickered. "He didn't seem as happy after he got off the phone with Sharon."

She looked pointedly at me. "For your information, Sharon is Melvin's wife and just happens to be a good friend of the suspect."

Irma returned her attention to Clair. "I guess Sharon's so mad she could spit. She kept insisting Helen's so nice, she wouldn't do such a thing."

Irma waved a curly fry at Clair. "Helen lied right off the bat. She insisted she hadn't been in Earl's office for months, but there was that cup still wet with coffee."

Clair nodded. " Even if she left the prints months ago—and nobody washed the cup—the coffee would've dried up."

Irma popped the fry into her mouth and chewed between words. "Sharon yelled so loud I could hear her through the phone. She swore Helen was playing Bingo with her on the night in question. Melvin kept repeating, 'Evidence doesn't lie.'"

I raised my hand to get her attention. "Irma, was there a coffee pot in Earl's office?"

Irma rolled her eyes. "I don't know. I suppose so, since there was coffee."

"It's just that I was at Earl's office the week before he died. I don't remember a coffee maker. In fact, he made a point of telling me he couldn't offer me coffee.

He didn't drink it because it's a drug."

Irma picked another curly fry. "Huh. She must have brought it with her."

She turned to Clair. "These are good fries. I'm coming back here. It's nice to have a new burger place in town. What's with the name, Bean Sprouts?"

Warming to a new topic, Clair held up the menu. "There's a whole page of healthy alternatives here. Look. Veggie-burgers, salads, bean sprouts to put on your burger."

"Clair." I interrupted. "Doesn't it seem odd Helen took a gun with her, and also brought a cup of coffee?"

"I guess. But who's to say what a murderer is thinking?" Clair smiled and pointed an index finger at me. "You're such a detective."

Still perusing the menu, Irma commented. "I don't think I'd like sprouts on my burger."

I slumped in the booth. "I'm heading home. Thanks for sharing the information with me."

A frown crossed Irma's face. "Don't tell anyone what I told you. Especially, anyone from the department. I could lose my job."

Having assured her of my discretion, I drove home repeating "It's over. They caught the killer. Don't read more into it."

Chapter Twenty-four

I stood on the front porch and fumbled my keys. Me and my imagination. Helen. I would never have suspected. That shows how much insight I have into the criminal mind.

Something furry brushed across my ankle causing me to jump and drop the keys. Bending down to retrieve them, I found myself looking at a black and white face with golden eyes. "You again?" The cat went back to circling my feet with his tail brushing teasingly across my shins.

"Why don't you go home?" Not only did I have a wild imagination and no insight into the criminal mind, I talked to cats.

He opened his mouth wide, letting out an earsplitting cry.

"Yikes. Are you hungry? Is that it?"

A low rumble seemed to be coming from his body as he sat down to rub the top of his head on my ankle.

"Okay, but just so you know, I'm not good at

caring for pets. Can't even take care of myself." I narrowed my eyes at the cat. "I'll feed you but you will stay outside."

I opened the door, stuck out my foot to keep the unwelcome visitor outside, and slipped into the house. In the kitchen, I poured a saucer of milk, then carried it to the steps. He didn't need an invitation. Milk splattered onto the step as the cat lapped, all the while purring loud enough for the neighbors to hear.

After watching him slurp for a minute, I became resigned to cat care. "I guess you'll need more than milk."

After I scooped up my keys and gingerly stepped over the cat, I hopped into the Chrysler and drove to the Grocery Mart.

Never having had a pet, I was stunned by the dietary selection, and stood rooted in the center of the aisle. Infinite varieties lined the shelves. There couldn't be enough cats in Evelynton to warrant all this. Don't they eat canned tuna or something? After reading the labels of at least a dozen cans, I chose four with pictures of cats that looked sort of like the one outside my house, and carried them to the checkout.

"Good evening. Did you find everything you need?" The curly haired check-out girl gave me a toothy grin and began passing each can over the scanner.

"Yep, just need the cat food. Um, do you have a cat, Candace?" With my keen investigative skills, I'd discovered her name on the tag she wore.

"No, but my grandma has seven." She looked up

from bagging the cans, to giggle. "Some people think she's strange. They call her the cat lady, but she loves her cats. They keep her company."

My wallet yielded a total of three dollars and twenty-eight cents, so I swiped my credit card. "Hmm. What does she feed them?"

"Oh, she buys fifty-pound bags of dry food. She couldn't afford to feed them special canned food like this. I bet your cat is one happy kitty."

"These are good? It's my first cat."

"Sure, all these are big sellers." She handed me the receipt and bag.

Carrying my purchases to the car, I couldn't help but think of the grandma with seven cats. Great, I'm a single woman and here I am with a cat—that I've been talking to. I will not be referred to as the cat lady. One cat, living in the box, outside. I'll feed him. That's all. Can't let him starve.

When I arrived home, the cat stood sentinel beside the empty saucer. He watched me expectantly as I stepped around him and walked inside.

I'd neglected to buy a cat bowl. Rummaging in the back of a lower cabinet yielded a dull, well-used pie tin. I spooned a couple globs of cat food into it and took it to the back porch. I was about to do the "Here kitty kitty" thing, but found him waiting on the step. "Pretty sure of yourself, aren't you?" He kept his eyes on the goal and attacked it as soon as I set it down.

One cat. And he stays outside.

Chapter Twenty-five

I hate it when people chat on their cell phones, not paying attention to where they're walking. But there I was with mine to my ear, almost colliding with a woman exiting Ava's. In my defense, Anita called as I stepped out of the car, and once she got going, it was impossible to cut in.

"You didn't seem convinced of Helen's guilt. You aren't about to start detecting, are you?"

I moved to the side and stood next to the building, out of the path of foot-traffic. "No, I won't be detecting. I'll accept the professional verdict. I know they have evidence, but it's hard for me to believe Helen's a killer. I can't say I really know her. Only met her that one time."

"Just trust our police department to do their job."

"You're right. We can't worry about it. Just let justice take its course. Personally, I want to forget about it and write—something peaceful."

"How's the book coming along?"

"Book? Oh, I've put it on hold for a while." I'd almost forgotten the fabricated novel. "I'm going into Ava's now to work on article ideas. I'll call you later." I clicked off.

Few customers frequented the coffee shop at this time of day, and I welcomed the solitude.

Settled with a cup of my favorite brew, I feverishly recorded ideas, until the chirp of my cell phone broke my concentration.

Should've turned it off.

It was a surprise to hear Wallace Binion's voice. "I have some information you can use."

"Information?" I didn't have a clue as to what he was referring.

"The New York City address of that classmate of yours. And a few numbers of current residents in the apartment building. Maybe give them a call and see if they remember him."

Paul Cooper. I'd pushed those suspicions out of my mind. "Wow, that's great Wallace. How did you—?"

"Called some people. Listen, I'll be out of town for the next few days. I'll leave the address for you. Lauren, no matter what you discover, wait for me. Don't do anything unless it's talking to the police."

"Okay. I'll... Wallace?" The line was dead.

I scooped up my stuff and made for the door, hoping to catch him before he left.

Within five minutes I pulled into my drive and jogged across the yard. I punched the doorbell. No answer. I rang it again, fully aware he was already gone. Wallace wasn't one to waste time.

My mailbox held a sticky note with the address and phone numbers. I plucked the note and read as I opened the door. I tossed my handbag on the end table, but it fell off. A cat occupied the spot.

"How'd you get in here? Back outside you go." He slipped through my grasp and jumped to the floor morphing into a black and white blur as all four feet went into motion. Claws clattered on the hardwood and he skittered across the room, disappearing under the sofa.

Crap.

Down on my hands and knees, I reached in as far as I could. Having come up empty, I stretched farther and swished my hand back and forth. Nothing. I got down on my stomach for one more try. This time, I grasped a paw, and slowly pulled the limp animal from his hiding place. Drawing him into my arms, I held him firmly and struggled to my knees. His warm body emitted a super-charged purr. My resolve slipped away.

"You can't stay here."

He twisted in my arms, and snuggled closer, pressing his head under my chin. The furry body vibrated, his heart beat next to mine.

Uh, oh.

~

Two hours and fifty dollars later, a selection of cat supplies sat on the back porch.

The cat curled up next to my feet while I worked at the computer. As soon as I powered it down and flipped on the television, he claimed my lap and spent the evening there.

I let him explore the house when I went to bed, but awoke the next morning with my feet pinned to the mattress. I propped myself up on my elbows and stared at the sleeping cat. As he raised a lazy head and blinked at me, I questioned the wisdom of this adoption. What do stray cats carry? Fleas, lice, tics, disease?

"Cat, you and I have to make a trip to the vet to get a checkup and shots."

After a lazy stretch, from his front toes to the tip of his tail, he jumped from the bed and stalked out of the room.

I showered and sat at the kitchen table expecting the cat to sit at my feet. When he didn't show, I went on a search, room by room.

"Here kitty kitty." Not a sight nor a sound of him.

Finally, I peeked under the sofa. A glint of light, reflected in a golden eye, revealed his hiding place. By lying flat on my stomach, again, and extending my arm as far as possible, I took hold of a paw and tugged until I got a grip on the cat, who seemed to be playing dead. Holding the lifeless body, I struggled to my feet. One golden eye opened.

"It's only a check-up and maybe a vaccination." Both eyes were now open. "Unless we go, you can't stay inside." He blinked.

I managed to maintain control while I gathered my keys and wrenched the Chrysler door open. Once inside, I released him to sit on the passenger seat.

The drive was easier than anticipated. He didn't

make a sound, didn't scratch me, or try to sit on my head. Safely parked in the veterinary clinic parking lot, I confidently turned to pick him up. Gone. I got on my knees to inspect the floor in the back seat, and then crawled over the seat to the cargo area. No cat. After five minutes, I located him under the front seat and began to pry him loose. He became all elbows, knees, and stretched out toes. I'd pull one paw free and three others would spread out and brace themselves against the mechanisms of the seat. By the time I'd loosed each appendage and got him out of the car, perspiration dripped into my eyes, and my shirt stuck to my back.

Inside, I spoke to the receptionist and took a place on a bench to wait our turn. The cat tucked his tail between his legs and his head under my arm, revealing only a ball of fur to others in the room.

Ten minutes later, we were called to the examining room. The cat willingly jumped onto the stainless steel table and allowed Dr. Barry to stroke his head.

"You say he's a stray?" Dr. Barry opened the cat's mouth. "Teeth are good."

"Yes."

Why is that cat so calm?

"He showed up at my house and wouldn't go away so I fed him and then he sort of moved inside."

Dr. Barry laughed. "That'll happen with cats." He turned the cat over, looked at his feet, picked him up, and said. "Well hello, Mason. We've been wondering where you went."

My head jerked up, full attention on the doctor. "Mason? You know him? Do you know who lost him?" My stomach twisted into a knot and my lips began to quiver.

The doctor placed Mason back on the table. "He used to belong to Fred Kissinger. Fred died, at ninety-five, a few months ago. The family went to clean out the house and said Mason just disappeared."

"Oh. I didn't know he had owners." I took a deep breath and squeaked. "I can take him to them." My fingers inched stealthily toward the cat. The door was only three feet away. I could grab him and make a run for it. Had I given the receptionist my full name?

"It's up to you." Dr. Barry said. "It looks to me like Mason is happy and healthy. The Kissingers were just going to take him to the shelter. They don't want him."

I snatched the cat from the table and croaked. "The shelter? No. I'll keep him. He chose me, after all."

Dr. Barry smiled and his eyes twinkled. "He sure did. I'm glad he's found himself a good home."

The doctor moved to a computer and with a few keystrokes, brought up what I guessed was Mason's file. "All his shots are up to date. I'm updating his address with the information you supplied this morning."

"Thank you." Mason struggled in my arms until I realized I was choking him. I loosened my grip and backed toward the door. "How much do I owe?"

"Not a thing today." Dr. Barry was still smiling. He had a great smile. "Just bring him in for his yearly check-up in January. We'll send you a reminder card.

Call me if you have any questions about his care."

"Thank you." I couldn't think of anything else to say, and was aware of a silly grin on my face. *When did I become so possessive of a cat?*

I walked to the car, holding my cat—*my cat*—against my chest. "Mason? What kind of name is that for a kitty?"

He purred.

We drove home. Mason fell asleep on the passenger seat and I hummed to a tune on the radio.

Chapter Twenty-six

The tinny ring of claws scratching the screen brought me to my feet. I obediently left my writing and trekked to the back porch. Mason stared at me through the screen door awaiting entrance. "You've sure made yourself at home in only three days." I opened the door and he pranced in, tail held high.

I returned to my work but hadn't finished a full paragraph before his warm body curled around my feet like a furry foot-warmer.

The shrill ring of the telephone startled me and I reached for the receiver. Mason lifted his head, grunted his complaint, and snuggled closer.

A throaty voice resonated through the line. "Hello, Lauren. Katherine Kennedy here, how are you?"

"Katherine, what a surprise. How's my favorite editor, and how's the gala life of the big city?"

"Grueling. I work sixty hours a week, no one appreciates me, and I love every minute of it."

"I was just thinking of you. I'm getting ready to send Michigan Christmas. Ahead of the deadline."

"That's great, Lauren. You can always be trusted to get your copy in on time, but that's not why I called. I have an offer you might be interested in. The company's scheduled brainstorming sessions for the coming year and we're inviting five of our top contributors. How does an all-expense paid trip to New York sound?"

Springing to my feet, I sent Mason rolling underneath the desk, and tipped the chair over. "Katherine, it sounds amazing. I'd love it."

I straightened the chair with my free hand. "When do you have in mind?"

"Next week. Meetings are Friday and Saturday. I'll book your ticket and hotel and email you the details."

"I can't wait. I'll start making arrangements to get freed up." Arrangements? Who was I kidding? It would require all the work of locking the door.

"By the way. The last time we talked you mentioned your interest in writing true crime. As much as I don't want to lose you to the book publishing world, I talked to my friend at Kendall House. They're opening a new brand dedicated to that genre, and will be open to new authors. He gave me a few tips."

"Really Katherine? That's so kind of you. I promise I won't quit writing for the magazine—even when I become a famous crime writer. What did he say?"

"They'll be interested if the subject sparks the imagination of the public. Something no one has written about or the public hasn't heard of. They don't want something that's been hashed over in the press. It would have to be presented in such a way as to draw the reader into the mind of the criminal. We're talking about personal interviews. You would want to get to him before anyone from the press gets there, to dig out his reasoning and motivation."

"I could do that." I'm not sure how, but I'd figure it out.

"As I think about it, Lauren, this just doesn't sound like you. It gives me the creeps. Do you think you'd want to interview a killer? Even if he was behind bars? And you'd have to hear the gruesome details. That would scare me to death."

"I guess it'd scare me, too. But it is what I've always wanted to do. At least, this gives me something to think about. I appreciate the information."

"Right now, I'm looking forward to the sessions in New York, and can't wait to get there."

I grabbed a pen to circle the dates on my calendar. Wait, I have a job. What will I tell Rarity? Only one work day. She'll understand.

I caught site of Mason staring at me from across the room. I have a cat. Maybe Anita will cat sit.

Unaware of the discussion buzzing inside my head, Katherine continued. "Wonderful. I look forward to seeing you. Bring some fresh ideas."

"I can't thank you enough. I'm so excited about the sessions." I clicked off.

Mason stalked up to sit at my feet, accusing me with an unblinking glare.

Crap.

"What am I going to do with you? How about if I leave you outside? Or I could lock you inside, and ask Anita to feed and check on you."

Mason turned his back to me, lifted his back leg, and proceeded to clean himself.

"I'll think of something."

I wandered into the kitchen and eyed the back porch. Could I lock the door into the house and prop the outside door open? Not a good idea. A doggy door? It would work for the weekend and be a relief in the future. No more letting the cat in and out at his every whim. When I'm gone, I could put his bed on the porch, and lock both the screen door and the inside kitchen door for security.

Mason finished his ablutions and returned his attention to me. "Don't worry, Mason, I'm not leaving you stranded. In fact, I'm going out to buy you a present."

~

I came back from the hardware store and dropped the package on the floor for Mason's inspection. "Look. It's perfect—a pet door for screens. All I have to do is install it."

After studying the instructions for ten minutes, I called Anita, who reported she'd be happy to check in on Mason while I was away. Unfortunately, she didn't know anything about home projects, and said her husband knew even less. "Clair's good at fixing things. She even has a toolbox. I'll call her and we'll be over. Between the three of us, it'll be a snap."

~

It wasn't a snap, and Clair did all the work, but by afternoon, we admired a working pet door.

As soon as the pounding ceased, Mason approached to inspect his private entrance, poking it with his paw and nudging it with his nose. He then made his way outside, turned around, and stepped back in.

"Smart cat." Clair packed her tools and plopped into a chair.

Anita beamed. "Look at him. He already knows how to use it." She applauded Mason and turned to me. "Don't worry about a thing. Go to New York and have fun. I'll be over every day to feed Mason and lavish him with attention."

I high-fived Anita, not wanting to admit I'd considered canceling the trip if my cat wasn't provided for.

~

Birds sang, and my world was glorious as I jumped out of bed the next morning. With an abundance of energy, I put on sneakers and slipped out onto the street for a jog. Cool, clear air filled my lungs. I'd never seen the sun so bright. After four blocks of jogging, I rounded the corner and ran full speed, all the way home, to check my email.

All travel information had arrived. Thank you, Katherine. I was scheduled to fly out Friday morning, arriving in time for a luncheon and the first session. Her note read, "I couldn't book a reasonable return flight until Monday morning. Hope it's okay."

Was it okay? Only the most exciting news I'd

received all year—make that five years. Window shopping, eating in great restaurants—if only a salad. Donning my city clothes!

I scooped up Mason and danced across the room. He fought me and jumped down just in time for me to answer the phone.

Chapter Twenty-seven

"Lauren. Guess what." My friend yelled.

I pulled the receiver away from my ear. "Good morning, Clair."

Had to tell you the news. Irma called to say they let Helen Peters go. She had an alibi. Sharon wouldn't let Melvin rest until he checked it out."

"An alibi? When did that come about?"

"Sharon made Melvin talk to everyone who was at the Bingo hall on the night of the murder. It was the annual Bingo Marathon and Helen played all night. Everybody swore they saw her, and she didn't leave until six a.m."

I pulled out a chair from the table and sank into it. "I thought he was sure. What about the evidence?"

"According to Irma, they'll have to sift through it all again. Oh, and this is weird; the hairs found on the body had been cut off, not pulled out. They knew because of no bulb. There's supposed to be a bulb on the end when a hair falls out or was pulled, but not if it was cut."

"Cut? Maybe the hairs don't mean anything. Maybe he picked them up from Patsy, since she works at the salon. I find somebody else's hair on my clothes all the time, and all I do is answer the phone." I leaned back and watched Mason. He twirled in tight circles, chasing his tail.

"Irma said Melvin was so disheartened, she got brave and mentioned your question about the coffee maker. They took another look at the cup."
Huh. Irma had been listening, after all. "What did they find?"

"Just like you said, no coffee maker. They don't know where the cup came from, but it doesn't match any at Helen's house or the nursing home. Melvin's thinking the lab messed up on the prints."

Mason broke out of the tail chasing circle to gallop through the dining room and leap onto the window sill. "Um, any other suspects? How about someone with a grudge against Earl?"

"Not as far as Irma knows. But she said Melvin has everybody working overtime."

"I hope—" An insistent rapping interrupted me. "I have to go. Someone's at the door. Talk to you later."

I put the phone down and peeked through the window before pulling the door open.

Deputy Farlow stood at attention on the porch, hands at his sides. "Good morning, Ms. Halloren. May I come in? I have a few more questions for you." I looked down at my sweats, longing for the shower, but stepped back to let him by.

He walked three steps into the room, pivoted to face me, and remained silent while I closed the door.

Let's get this off on the right foot. I smiled. "I heard you weren't feeling well, Deputy Farlow. I'm glad you're back on your feet. What can I do for you?"

His expression remained stony, while color crept into his neck and cheeks. "I'll tell you what you can do for me. You can give me the truth."

My mouth opened and snapped shut. I could think of nothing to say.

"You denied owning a gun, but the paperwork says differently." Farlow read from his notebook. "I think your exact words were 'Steak knives are the closest thing to a weapon in this house. I hate guns.' Is that how you remember it?"

Me and my dumb sense of humor. "I guess so, but—"

"Imagine my surprise when I discovered there is a Smith & Wesson 442 registered in your name. In the state of Florida."

I pushed hair from my face, shook my head, and opened my mouth.

Farlow wasn't ready for me to speak. "You want to change your answer? Is this weapon still in your possession?"

My knees began to buckle, so I slid into the nearest chair. "I'm sorry, I can explain. When you asked me about a weapon, I'd forgotten all about the gun."

I folded my hands, trying to appear honest.

I am honest.

"When you asked, I believed I was telling the truth. I just forgot. You see, my husband was killed in a drive-by shooting, in Florida. I couldn't stand looking at the gun and packed it away after that, and sealed the box. That was over five years ago."

Deputy Farlow squinted at me and folded his arms across his chest. He cleared his throat and took a deep breath. "I'm sorry for your loss. I understand it must've been a trying time, and you might have forgotten about storing it. Let's open the box and get the weapon now. I'll take it down to the office to be checked out."

Uh, oh.

I clenched my hands tighter and inhaled deeply. "I. I was thinking about the murder the other day and got scared because I live alone. Well, that's when I remembered the gun. I got it out of the box, for protection, and put it in my purse."

I pried my hands apart and reached into my handbag. Deputy Farlow took a step back as I pulled out the gun. His right hand went to his own weapon, still in the holster at his side.

I let my gun dangle from two fingers while I offered it to him. "I'm sorry. When I remembered the gun, I forgot that I told you I didn't have one." My story was so convoluted, even I didn't believe it.

"It's loaded?"

I nodded once. "Yes sir, it is."

Without taking his eyes off me, Farlow pulled a plastic baggy from his pocket, let me drop my handgun into it, and slid the whole thing into his jacket pocket.

"Ms. Halloren, I'm taking this downtown. I'm going to ask you not to leave town until I talk to you again. Depending on what we find, I may have more questions."

"Yes, sir." I nodded and then shook my head. "I won't be going anywhere. Well, I have a trip planned, but not until the end of next week. I'll be sure to talk to you first."

"Right. I'll get back to you." He tipped his hat and left.

What had I gotten myself into? Suddenly my throat was so dry I couldn't swallow, and I trotted to the kitchen for a glass of water. Always a step ahead of me, Mason leapt to the counter and to the window sill. I scratched his ears and gazed through the window. Wallace's car sat in his driveway.

Thank you, God.

I ran out of the house, cutting through the yard to his back door.

Chapter Twenty-eight

Wallace stood at his kitchen counter, dishtowel in hand, when I showed up at his screen door.

"Lauren, good to see you. How's everything?" He threw the towel over his shoulder and held the door open for me.

"I'm so glad you're home, everything is a mess. I thought I'd be bored in this little town, but instead, my life has been turned upside down." I paced around the kitchen and drew in a deep breath. "The police released Helen Peters. She has an alibi."

"So I heard. Is that a problem?"

I stopped and looked into his eyes. "Now I'm a murder suspect."

A smile spread across his face and he laughed. "What? You aren't serious."

With a closer look at my expression, he sobered mid-laugh. "What makes you think so?" Pulling out a chair from the kitchen table, he said, "Sit and tell me about it."

Wallace maintained an unblinking gaze as I explained about the gun, my forgetfulness, and inadvertent lie.

He lowered himself into the chair across from me and closed his eyes for a moment. "Repeat that last part."

I painstakingly explained about remembering the gun, loading it, and putting it in my handbag, only to have to surrender it to Officer Farlow.

Wallace ran a hand through his hair and blew out a breath through his teeth. "Have you fired the weapon recently?"

I was happy to reply. "No, not in ages, since Marc insisted I take lessons. It's been boxed away, more than five years."

"Good, they'll discover it hasn't been fired and check the caliber of the bullet, which probably won't be a match. Most likely, they'll return it to you in a few days."

"Do you think you should you be carrying a loaded gun?"

"I'm very careful." Did he think I was a child? Wallace narrowed his eyes, in an expression I read as doubt. I rushed on with my explanation. "I need it. With Helen exonerated, the killer is still loose. I'm sure Paul Cooper knows I've been asking questions. He glares at me every time I see him. What if he's the killer and he comes after me?"

Wallace nodded. "Have you mentioned your suspicions to the authorities?"

"No." I let my shoulders slump. "My own friends think I'm crazy, I can't go to the police saying I don't remember him and he gives me mean looks."

"You're probably right about that." Wallace leaned back and leveled his gaze at me. "What have you discovered about Cooper?"

I squirmed. "Not much. I haven't had time to look into the information you gave me. Things have been busy at my house and I thought the murder was solved."

Wallace raised his eyes to the ceiling for a moment. "When they return the gun, don't carry it in your purse. Keep it in a drawer at home and lock it in the glove compartment when you go out."

"Wallace, I know how to use it." I began to defend myself.

"The last time you fired it was five years ago?"

"It was, but...." I choked under Wallace's steady gaze. "Okay, I guess it would be safer."

Wallace visibly relaxed and smiled. "When you get it back, why don't I take you to a shooting range and give you a refresher course?"

~

A week later, Officer Farlow returned my gun, stating it wasn't a match for the murder weapon. As soon as he left, I glanced over at Wallace's empty driveway. With only a tinge of guilt, I reloaded the Smith & Wesson and slipped it into my handbag.

Chapter Twenty-nine

One call to Anita and I would be on my way to the big city, happily leaving Evelynton behind.

"I'm off to the airport." I scanned my checklist.

"You'll find the spare key under the flower pot on the front porch. Take it and I'll get it back when I see you."

Mason jumped into my arms for a last cuddle. I carried him to the back porch and made sure the doors were locked.

At a table near the front door, the slip of pink paper caught my eye. I hadn't even looked at Paul Cooper's New York address since the day Mason moved in. Troubling suspicions had been shoved to the back of my mind. Maybe that's the way it should be. Life is easier without mysteries.

Tucking my handbag under my arm, I took one step out, stepped back in, and grabbed the note. It would be easy enough to check out, while in New York. After I shoved the note into my handbag, I realized I was about to make a big mistake. The suitcase dropped to the floor, and I pulled the Smith & Wesson out of my bag. Carrying a gun onto the plane was not a good idea. I hurried to the linen closet and shoved the weapon under a stack of towels.

The drive was easy, although I was forced to exceed the speed limit to arrive on time. After depositing the car in long-term parking, I boarded and found my aisle seat next to a plump woman in a shiny black running suit. Her focus remained on her paperback, and by the time we were in the air, she'd slouched to the side, snoring softly. I snuggled down in my seat and pulled out the flight magazine wishing I could sleep as easily.

It seemed only a minute later that the pilot announced our imminent arrival at JFK. My pulse pounded and I stretched for a view of the city through the window. Sun glistened off buildings as our plane circled the airport. I gripped the armrests for the touchdown and bounced up, with the rest of the passengers, as soon as the plane rolled to a stop. In my excitement, I barely noticed the usual aggravation of the baggage claim and locating the hotel shuttle. Before long, I was gawking at the view from my tenth floor hotel room.

I had just enough time to change, and resisted the urge to dive onto the king size bed to stretch out among multiple pillows. Instead, I pulled a dress from my garment bag, changed into my city pumps, and ran to snag an elevator.

Waitresses served lunch as I entered the

conference room.

~

I wish I could describe the enthralling session, but my thoughts often strayed to the address on the slip of pink paper. Should I phone the current residents or knock on their doors?

At dinner, I calculated the cost of a taxi ride to Paul Cooper's apartment building. We were finally released, late in the evening, and I collapsed into bed, not opening my eyes until the wake-up call Saturday morning.

Sometime during the first break, I noticed the age discrepancy. The other writers in the room were at least ten years my senior. This didn't help my dedication to purpose. My career of homey magazine writing had run its course. I longed for bigger, more exciting writing topics in my future.

During the afternoon meeting, Katherine asked me a question I didn't hear because of my wandering thoughts. I had to apologize, and a guilty conscience forced me to double my efforts at concentration.

On Saturday evening, all meetings finished, I returned to my room with Maps open on my phone. After assessing the cash in my wallet, I planned the taxi ride to the apartment building after breakfast on Sunday.

Chapter Thirty

My plate stacked with everything from the breakfast buffet, I selected a table near the window. When I'd stuffed in the last bite, I tried to enjoy the atmosphere—white linen tablecloths, friendly waiters, no gossip—with no luck.

The excitement of the chase wouldn't let me rest. After tossing my napkin on the plate, I strode through the lobby in search of a cab.

Before long, I gripped my seatbelt and braced myself against the door, as the green and white cab darted through traffic. How quickly I'd become accustomed to small town drivers.

When the car came to an abrupt stop, I pried my hand from the armrest, paid the fare, and stepped onto the sidewalk. The drab, gray brick building before me was austere by Evelynton standards, only revealing traces of life at the windows. Here and there, a windowsill held a flower pot, lace curtains fluttered in the breeze, or a face gazed at the street.

I climbed the steps to the front door, grateful to find the window free of fingerprints and the foyer swept clean. Someone cared about these apartments.

A row of fifteen brass mailboxes hung in the foyer, with an intercom button centered on each box. I would need a resident to unlock the door leading into the building. Noting Paul's former apartment number—303—I began with the adjacent box in hopes someone might have known him.

The name Edwards was printed on apartment 301. I pushed the intercom. No answer. I pushed it again and waited. Still no answer. Not to be discouraged, I chose the next mailbox in the row, Marasovitch at number 302. This one got an immediate response.

"Yeah?" barked the speaker.

Not sure if the gruff voice was male or female, I began cautiously. "Hello? My name is Lauren Halloren, I wonder if I could ask you a few questions about a former tenant."

"What do you want?" Still no clue as to gender.

I leaned closer to the intercom. "I want to ask you about someone who lived on your floor about six years ago."

"Can't help you." I heard the intercom click off. Okay, thank you.

I tried apartment 304, punching the button several times with no response. Why had I assumed everybody would be home, and agreeable?

I moved on to the second floor, selecting the button for 201, Marino.

No answer. No one home. I kicked the wall with

the toe of my shoe. Did I really want to spend the whole day on this? What if no one remembered Paul Cooper?

I took a deep breath, blew it out, and pushed 202, Alcott. "Yes, hello." This was a cheerful voice.

Encouraged, I rushed through my request. "Hello. Mr. Alcott? I'm sorry to bother you. I'm in town for a few days and trying to track down someone who used to live in this building, in apartment 303. I wonder if you knew him."

"No bother. What's this person's name? Mrs. Twite lives in 303." I knew Mr. Alcott would be helpful.

"Paul Cooper. He lived in 303 about six years ago."

"Hmm." I waited hopefully. "I don't recall the name, but I've only lived here for three or four years. I moved here from Virginia to be near my daughter. No, sorry. I don't think I can help you."

Shoot. I raised my voice. "Is there anyone in the building who has lived here more than six years? Someone who might remember the previous tenants?"

After a pause long enough to make me wonder if Mr. Alcott had deserted, he said, "Oh, mercy me. There's, um no. Oh yes. Maybell Abernathy. She's been here years and years." A static filled chuckle sounded over the intercom. "She knows everybody who ever lived in this building. You should talk to her."

I pressed both hands on the wall and leaned close to the intercom. "Abernathy? Would she be in apartment 203?"

"Yes, right down the hall from me. Doesn't get out much, and keeps up with everyone's business."

I pushed away from the wall. Yes! "Would she be home right now?"

"Oh, I would think so. She's in her eighties. Almost always home. Unless her niece comes to take her to the doctor. She'll tell you all about your friend."

Mr. Alcott was so nice, I leaned close to the intercom, and used my sweetest voice. "It's difficult to hear over the intercom. Could you buzz me in so I can knock on her door?"

"No." How quickly a mood can change. "I couldn't do that, seeing as I don't know you. What if you're a thief or something?"

Hmmph. "No problem. You're very wise. Well, thank you for your time. I'll call on Mrs. Abernathy and see if she knows my friend Paul. Goodbye, Mr. Alcott."

I think I heard him say "Good day to you" as I pushed 203.

No one answered. I pushed it again and counted to twenty, wondering how long it would take an eighty year old woman to get to the intercom. What were the chances that today she'd be out? I may not be cut out to be an investigator. I turned and looked out through the window in the front door, my eyes drawn to a green and black, Starbucks sign. I'd taken one step in that direction when a soft, breathy voice sounded from the intercom.

Chapter Thirty-one

"Hello, who is it?"

I pivoted so fast my hair slapped me in the face. "Mrs. Abernathy, I'm Lauren Halloren. Mr. Alcott suggested I talk to you about a man who used to live in the apartment above yours."

"Mr. Alcott sent you? Just a minute, I'll let you in."

A buzzer sounded and I heard a click as the latch released. Guilt pulled at me as I grabbed the door handle. I didn't like deceiving a little old lady, but desperately wanted to talk to someone face to face. Bypassing the elevator, I took the steps two at a time. The door to 203 opened, revealing a softly wrinkled face, surrounded by thin white curls that didn't quite conceal a pink scalp.

I looked down into her pale blue eyes. She stood four feet tall, at best. "Hello, Mrs. Abernathy, I'm Lauren."

"Hello dear. Please come in. Would you care for a cup of tea? I made it just before you rang." She backed away from the door and shuffled to a rocking chair.

"Thank you, I'd love some." I perched on a diminutive upholstered chair, matching the rocker Mrs. Abernathy occupied. A small round table separated us.

From my seat, I could see most of the apartment—bedroom, efficiency kitchen and sitting room, where we were now. Lace curtains, tied with pastel ribbon, revealed window shades raised to let the sunshine fill the room.

"Do you remember Paul Cooper? He lived in 303, a few years back."

Mrs. Abernathy poured the tea, her face scrunching into a beautiful smile. "I remember him well. Such a nice young man. He used to pick up groceries for me and help if something needed to be fixed in the apartment." She puckered her lips and blew on her tea. "The super takes care of repairs now, as he should, but Paul would just come in as soon as he was home from work, and ask how he could help." She tested her tea. "I miss his friendly face."

Her eyebrows drew together, adding more wrinkles. "He left without saying goodbye. It wasn't like him. I thought he must have been so grief-stricken when his friend was killed, he up and left." Mrs. Abernathy studied the contents of her cup. "He never wrote. I thought Paul would write." She glanced up at me. "You young people don't do that anymore, do you? Letter writing is a lost art. Everyone emails or texts. If you don't have a computer or one of those smartphones, you're out of luck."

I had to agree. "I guess we don't write letters

much." I set my teacup on the table. "Did you say a friend of Paul's was killed?"

"Yes, such a tragedy. Roger Hicks was the man's name, although I wasn't convinced that was his real name. Hicks. A homeless man Paul took in. Paul was like that, didn't think anything at all of talking to vagrants loitering on the street." Mrs. Abernathy's white curls bobbed as she shook her head. "He invited Roger right into his apartment. Cleaned him up and put him to work. I don't mind telling you, I didn't like it one bit, at first. But Roger turned out to be a decent sort. Paul even taught him to do some of the repair work. Fixed my jammed windows and they slid up and down real easy after that. He was alright."

I pulled a notebook from my bag and recorded the name. "And Roger was killed?"

"Yes, I read about it in the morning paper. They found him in an alley. Thieves probably got him and dragged him back there. Too bad."

Mrs. Abernathy put a hand to her chin and turned to look at the china cabinet. "I cut out the notice. It's here somewhere." She turned to point at the bookshelf. "Yes, I put it in the back of my Bible. I don't know why I saved it. Guess I thought Paul would want it when he came back. You can have it, if you want." She pulled the Bible from the shelf.

I accepted the flattened clipping. "It was after Roger was killed, that Paul moved out?"

"Yes, the same day they found him. Found his ID card in his pocket." Mrs. Abernathy tipped her head. "I remember when Paul helped him get that."

Horns blared outside the window and the breeze carried in a scent of exhaust fumes, while Mrs. Abernathy recounted her memories. "Paul was home in the morning. His apartment was right above mine so I could hear him. I thought he must have called in sick to work that day because he was still home at eleven-thirty." She sighed heavily. "I was going to fix him a nice cup of tea when he came down to talk, but he never came. I even called on the phone but he didn't answer." She shrugged. "The next day, he was gone— even left his furniture. The super said he left a note saying to go ahead and rent the apartment."

Mrs. Abernathy finished her tea and set the cup aside. "I was surprised Paul didn't stay around to arrange burial. I suppose they gave Roger a pauper's funeral since he didn't have anyone." She folded her arms across her stomach and rocked back and forth. "I don't understand why Paul left like that. I wonder where he is."

"He's back in his hometown." I pulled my phone from my bag. "I have a picture of him." I scrolled through the images, and finding the one of Paul, handed it to Mrs. Abernathy. "He's standing at the back, behind the two women."

Mrs. Abernathy squinted and adjusted her glasses. "Wait, let me focus. My eyes aren't what they used to be, even with these expensive glasses. Cost me a fortune."

She leaned close and studied the image before raising her eyes to mine. "But that isn't Paul." She turned the phone toward me. "That man is Roger

Hicks. It's been five or six years and he's all dressed up, but it's Roger." She shook her head. "Well, I declare, I thought he was dead."

My heart began beating so fast I struggled to catch my breath. Pieces of the puzzle clicked together. Roger Hicks murdered Paul and stole his identity.

Mrs. Abernathy's phone rang and she raised a finger. "Just a minute." She reached for the receiver and, after a few words of greeting, covered the mouthpiece to whisper, "It's my niece."

I stood and whispered. "I should be going. Thank you so much for your time, and the tea. I'll let myself out."

She kept her hand over the mouthpiece. "Goodbye dear. When you catch up with Paul, tell him to write to me." She turned to chat with her niece, and I slipped into the hall.

I barely remember sprinting down the stairs and out to the street to flag a taxi.

Chapter Thirty-two

The door swung open and I inhaled the fragrance of furniture polish and fabric softener. Home. I dropped my luggage on the floor and ran to open the back door to find Mason. He sat erect, in the center of the porch, as if expecting me at that moment. I scooped him into my arms and held him close, feeling his body vibrate.

"Did you miss me? It's nice to have someone welcome me home."

He stayed in my arms as I stepped back into the kitchen, then he pushed out, and set off to explore the house.

I looked through the window toward Wallace's house—no sign of him—and left voice mail messages for Anita and Clair before collapsing on the sofa. Having finished his exploration, Mason performed a graceful leap from the floor to my lap, made three circles, and laid down for a nap.

"No sleeping." I lifted his chin. "What do you

think? Should I go to the police? That's probably the smartest thing." Mason blinked. "But that means no scoop, maybe no book. I've gone this far, why not get the whole story, right from the impostor's mouth? I'll catch him alone. Maybe he'll talk to me. I might convince him he'll be famous when I write his story."

Mason leapt to a chair and sat with his back to me. I felt a sudden urge to defend myself. "Don't be silly. I know what I'm doing, and need to get started before I change my mind."

I jumped off the sofa, grabbed my keys, and retrieved the Smith & Wesson from the closet. With it securely in my handbag, I pushed aside the butterflies of concern, and left the house.

Scenes from *Perry Mason* and *Murder She Wrote* played in my head, as I drove. Pulling to the curb a block from Cooper's house, I surveyed the area. No vehicles in sight. I straightened my shoulders and marched to the front door. Just as my finger touched the doorbell, loud creaking and groaning sounded from nearby, causing me to gasp and stifle a scream. The garage door had begun its ascent, so I did my best to blend into the shadows.

An older model black sedan backed into the street, my prey at the wheel. I let him drive half a block before I ran for the Chrysler.

Paul seemed unaware of the vintage station wagon tailing him, as he drove out of town, and merged onto the interstate. I maintained a safe distance, keeping him in sight. Twenty minutes on the road, and I'd begun to wonder about my gas supply when Paul took the Warrenton exit. I followed until he pulled into a public lot, and I drove past to find a space on the street.

Slumped down in my seat, I watched in the mirror as he got out and proceeded into an alley. I abandoned the Chrysler, power-walked to the entrance, and peeked into the alley in time to see Paul enter a warehouse. I jogged along the side of the alley to within six feet, crouched low, and crept to the door. Letters painted on the window in the door, read God Sheltered Recovery House.

A quick look into the window revealed a dimly lit hallway. It appeared empty, so drawing a deep breath, I gently eased the door open, and slipped in. I tiptoed as quickly as possible to another door, with a larger window. Taking shallow breaths and willing my heartbeat to slow, I moved to peer through the window.

Chapter Thirty-three

The harsh glare from an industrial lighting fixture illuminated the wood shop. Saws, drills, and hammers, rested on wooden tables. Sawdust and wood scraps littered the concrete floor. Thinking Paul—or Roger—had proceeded to a room at the back, I applied pressure to the door handle, but stilled as he reappeared from the side, carrying a length of wooden molding. He proceeded to a work bench about twenty feet from the door. I held my breath while he pulled up a stool, and picked up a square of sandpaper.

His vigorous sanding created enough noise to cover the sound of my entrance. The crunching of each step echoed in my ears, but I was able to approach to within a few feet, while he worked intently. Finally sensing my presence, he lifted his eyes, startled.

"Hey, Lauren, this is a surprise. What brings you here?" His words were pleasant, his eyes wary, and his hands still sanding.

"Hello, Roger. I just returned from New York, talked to your neighbor. I know the truth."

He froze, his eyes boring into mine. Then he gave a short chuckle. "What do you mean by that?" He returned his attention to the board, methodically moving the sandpaper back and forth. "Is this some kind of joke? Perry put you up to it?"

Pushing down an urgent desire to run, I forgot my preplanned script and spewed out the facts. Belatedly, I thought to scan the area for potential weapons, taking note of hammers and screwdrivers. I imagined him picking up the board and flinging it at me. Would I jump to the side?

What was I doing here? Clenching my teeth to keep from shaking, I slowly slid my hand inside my shoulder bag, searching for the reassuring touch of the gun.

Calmer, I continued. "I met Mrs. Abernathy. Do you remember her? She was quite fond of Paul. I showed her your picture. Imagine her surprise when she saw you—alive."

"What picture?" He spat out the words, dropped the sandpaper, and gripped the board tight enough to turn his knuckles white.

"From the reunion. Don't you remember? You tried to avoid it but I managed to get a couple snapshots."

His chest expanded in deep breaths before he retrieved the sandpaper, and returned to the methodical back and forth motion.

"Mrs. Abernathy read about your death in the

newspaper, but it was Paul's body they found, wasn't it? She said Paul was good to you. Why'd you do it? For his money? His identity? Or was that an afterthought?"

What am I doing? He could swing that board at me before I had a chance to aim my gun. I slid my right foot an inch back and followed with my left.

"And wasn't Paul the only friend you had?" Roger's face flushed and his breathing seemed labored. I glanced around, planning an escape, but the strangest thing happened. Roger sort of deflated, as though someone had let air out of a balloon.

He dropped the molding and bent over, burying his face in his hands. Not knowing whether to talk or to run, I waited in silence.

It was an old, weary man who finally lifted his head. Face wet with tears and vacant eyes. His hoarse voice barely audible. "I was a drunk, living on the street, digging in garbage cans for food.

Paul found me in the alley behind his building and tried to get me to go to a shelter, but I told him to keep out of my business." He wiped his eyes with the back of his hand. "I knew if I went to the shelter, they wouldn't let me drink and they'd start hammering me to dry out."

He took a quick breath and steeled his face. "I thought he'd go away, but he sat down on a box in the alley and talked. Not about anything in particular, just talk—the weather, the birds." A faint smile tugged at his mouth. "The new city buses. I hadn't had a real conversation in a long time. It was nice. He knew when I was tired of talking, and he left."

Roger ran his hand over his face and continued with more energy. "A day or two later, when I was making my rounds, he was in the alley waiting for me. He had a McDonald's bag with a couple of cold burgers in it. Said he bought too many and couldn't eat them." The smile grew as he spoke. "I believed him. Later I learned he never ate fast food. A real health nut."

Roger sighed and sat up straighter as the heavy burden of secrecy lifted. "Anyway, Paul came back every night to talk and bring me a burger. Pretty soon he convinced me to sleep in his spare room. Me, as dirty as I was. I hadn't even thought of a bath in a year. My own room and a real bed. It was nice. So I slept there at night. I'd leave in the morning and walk the streets begging for money to spend on whiskey or whatever booze I could get. But I went back every night."

Roger visibly relaxed, so I released my grip on the gun. He looked at me for the first time since he'd begun his story. "It started to sink in that I had a home. I was welcome. There was one person in the world glad to see me. He told me about his life, his mother's death and his father's dementia. He didn't have any family since his divorce."

"Pretty soon, Paul convinced me to change my ways. I didn't drink as much because I spent most evenings talking to him. One day he took me downtown to a clinic and convinced me to go in. I still don't know how he did it. I got dried out and went back to live with Paul. He found odd jobs for me around the apartment building, doing minor repairs.

Then I got a job bagging groceries."

Roger squeezed his eyes shut and sucked in a breath. "One day Paul didn't show up at the apartment." The tears had returned. "He didn't come home all night. Next day, I went looking for him, traced his route to the office where he worked, all the way into the city, and started back. I looked down every alley and in every vacant building."

Roger's voice became stronger and angry. "I found him beat to death, behind a deserted building. I sat down and cried. Stayed with him most of the night."

Roger raised his fist and shouted. "The only person who cared about me was gone. He was good. He didn't deserve to die like that."

I jumped and gripped the gun.

His voice dropped to a whisper. "That was the way I thought I'd die. I almost bought a bottle to take away the pain, but I didn't. I could hear him, 'I spent too much time on you to watch you go back to being a wreck. You owe your life to me.'"

Roger's face relaxed. "So I made a decision in that alley. Paul loved Evelynton and talked about going back, and becoming a real estate agent. I decided I'd live the life he would have—if he'd had the chance."

I removed my hand from my bag, away from my gun, and breathed in my first full breath since I'd entered the room. "And you did. I don't know how you managed it."

Roger stepped off the stool and stood in front of the bench. "I changed clothes with him, took his ID, and gave him mine. Roger Hicks was dead—and good riddance. Paul Cooper was alive."

He leaned against the bench, resting his hands on his hips as he boasted. "It was easy, I knew where he kept all his papers and cleaned out the checking account. I wrote a letter of resignation from his job— typed it and didn't sign it. They didn't care. He was just a number to them."

Roger paced back and forth in front of the bench. "That little old busybody was the only person who might cause a problem, so I packed up and moved out of the apartment. Lived in a little town in southern Indiana for a while, took the real estate course, and got my license. I came here, and I was Paul Cooper."

"You didn't worry someone might guess?"

He leaned toward me with a lopsided smile. "Nope. People want to believe what you tell them. I recognized a lot of faces from the yearbook and others just offered their names. Paul told me all kinds of high school stories and after so many years, nobody thinks it strange if you forget the details."

"It's been a good life." Roger's gaze swept the room. "I found this place, a half-way house where I can help other guys like me. I teach them to work with wood, and they give the things they build to the needy. I help them make something of themselves."

Roger stopped and looked at me with narrowed eyes. "You figured it out. How did you know?" He didn't wait for an answer. "The time in Evelynton has been better than all the years I lived before. I have a real life."

Despair crumpled his face as he leaned on the

table and lowered himself onto the stool. "But that's over now. You'll tell the police. My wife." He looked up at me. "Give me time to tell Missy, myself. She trusts me. This will destroy her."

His last words were muffled because he'd slumped over again, his head in his hands.

I remained rooted in place, legs aching from standing, thoughts whirling through my head. How can I destroy this man's life? Is he telling the truth? Is he lying? His story agreed with everything Mrs. Abernathy shared with me.

I don't know how long I stood before finding my voice. "I won't tell anyone. I'm not sure what good it would do. It's up to you to be truthful with your wife."

I backed toward the door. "I don't know what I would do in your place. I'm going home and forget all about it." That was a lie. I'd never forget.

Cool night air hit me in the face as I burst into the alley and ran to the Chrysler. I rolled down the windows, and drove into the setting sun, toward home. Relief seemed to be carried in along with the breeze. I wasn't crazy, Paul Cooper was indeed an impostor. Roger Hicks had assumed his identity. I broke through the Evelynton city limits and followed the street lights down Main Street.

From a parking spot outside the police station, I stared at shadowed figures moving inside the illuminated windows. Could I destroy a man's life— even a false one? Roger hadn't killed Paul. Would it be my finger that sent him back to being Roger Hicks— homeless alcoholic? Would I be the one to destroy his new life?

A brief gust of country music drifted from a passing carload of kids, while I made up my mind. I maneuvered the station wagon onto Main Street and guided it home.

Chapter Thirty-four

All my energy had seeped away and fatigue drove me to the sofa. I sank into it, dropping my bag on the floor. Roger's sorrow had drained me as if it'd been my own. He'd stolen Paul's identity, but who'd been hurt? What good would it do to inform the police?

True, the news would draw media attention and this was the story I'd always wanted to write. So much for my ticket out of here. I'm not tough enough.

I snuggled into the cushions and rested my head on the back of the sofa. "Mason, where are you when I need a cuddle?" Did I leave him outside? He's probably chasing moths.

I was about to force myself up from the sofa to turn on a lamp when a throaty growl reverberated near the front door. I searched the shadows until my eyes focused on the furry ball, huddled under the corner table. Golden eyes reflected the limited light. "Here kitty, kitty. What are you doing under there?"

Another growl bubbled up from deep within the cat. He didn't acknowledge me, his attention riveted to the staircase. My stomach clenched and threatened to erupt as I recalled the unlocked back door. How could I have been so careless? I slowly turned in the direction of Mason's gaze. The half-light revealed a shadowy figure and the metallic glint of a gun.

Gasping for air, I slid to the floor and my shoved hand inside my bag, searching for my weapon. I tugged it free and swung it toward the intruder. I knew I should order him out of my house with a commanding voice, but words wouldn't come.

Before I uttered a sound, a shot rang out. I ducked as glass shattered behind me, and raised my head in time to see the shooter stumble down the stairs. Shafts of moonlight afforded glimpses of the dark clad figure bolting toward the kitchen. The screen door slammed.

Pulse pounding, I scrambled to my feet, and ran through the dining room and kitchen, reaching the back door as he was tackled and taken to the ground.

"Oh, for gosh sakes!" Wallace exclaimed, after he'd pinned the struggling figure and wrenched the gun from his hand. "What the heck do you think you're doing?"

I retrieved my cell, punched 911 to report the break-in, and ventured into the yard.

A screen door slammed next door. Clive ran out of his house and stood at the property line, his shotgun in his hands. After appraising the situation, he turned and stalked back inside his house.

Wallace held his prey with ease, so I edged closer. "The police are on the way."

"You won't believe this." Wallace glanced up from the wriggling trespasser. "Take a look."

I crouched down. The hood of the navy sweatshirt slipped off a mass of overly processed hair, revealing the pale face, etched with fear.

"Patsy Clooney?" I was stunned. "What are you doing here?"

Patsy ceased struggling, and Wallace pulled her into a sitting position.

She turned her face toward the alley and gazed into the night. "We needed money to go to Florida."

"Who needed money?" I strained to follow her gaze but saw nothing. The illumination of the street lights didn't extend to the alley. When I returned my attention to Patsy, her lips pressed into a tight, grim line.

I knelt beside Wallace and Patsy, while sirens wailed in the distance, drew closer, and went silent in front of the house.

~

Wallace helped me up from the ground, and we sat on the wooden steps to give statements to Officer Farlow. Another officer pulled Patsy's hands behind her back and snapped handcuffs in place. Her gaze searched the darkness one more time before she was led to the patrol car.

After Wallace finished his statement, he put a hand on my shoulder. "Give me a shout, if you need anything." I watched him saunter toward his house and fade into the shadows.

Farlow turned a page in his notebook. "Okay Ms. Halloren, let's take a look inside."

I followed as he flipped on the lights, and scanned each room—everything in its place until we reached the living room. Farlow inspected the broken window and scratched a few notes.

I picked up Mason, massaging his ears as I waited. "She was on the stairs when I saw her."

Finished with the window, Farlow appraised the floor. "What's this?"

"Looks like she found the closet under the staircase." The few boxes I'd stashed had been pulled out and ripped open, contents splayed across the floor.

"She couldn't have found anything of value. Just a few files and photographs from my late husband's last assignment."

The officer pushed the papers aside with his foot. "Show me the rooms upstairs."

I led the way to my bedroom and peeked in. "This is a relief. The dresser drawers are open but my clothes aren't even mussed."

"Uh. Huh." Farlow leaned in, took a cursory look around, and stepped back onto the landing. After glancing into the spare room and closets, he slid his pen into his shirt pocket. "You interrupted her before she could go through your stuff."

We reached the foot of the stairs to find Wallace hammering the final nails into place, securing plywood to cover the broken window. "That'll keep 'til you can replace it. I cleaned up the papers and put them back in the boxes. Do you want them back in the closet?"

"No, this is as good a time as any to toss them into the trash."

"I'll take care of it for you." He left through the back door.

Exhaustion had me longing for bed by the time Farlow finished his notes and stepped to the door. "If you discover anything missing, give us a call tomorrow. Lock up." He tipped his head toward the street. "You'll be safe now that she's in custody."

I glanced past him. The interior lights of the police cruiser illuminated Patsy in the back seat, looking as bewildered as a lost child.

Chapter Thirty-five

What's that noise? The telephone ringer pulled me from the depths of deep slumber. I reached out and patted the top of the end table until my hand came into contact with the phone.

"Hello?"

"I'm glad you're up. I couldn't wait to talk to you. Just got off the phone with Irma. She filled me in about the excitement at your house last night."

"Clair? I guess I fell asleep on the sofa." The weight of a sleeping cat slid off my hip as I swung my feet to the floor and struggled to get into a sitting position.

"Weren't you up? Should I call back in a little while?"

I rubbed my eyes open. "Um. No, it's okay. I'm awake."

"Girlfriend you sound a little groggy, but I can't wait. Congratulations, you're the hero. You apprehended the town thief and Earl's killer, at the same time."

"What are you talking about, Clair? Hold on, I think I need coffee." Keeping the phone to my ear, I pushed up from the sofa and wandered to the kitchen, drawn to the early morning sunlight streaming through the windows.

"Irma told me all about it. She said you found Patsy in your house, ran after her and pounced on her when she tripped in the yard. Then you held her until the police came. Good for you, girl. Wish I could have seen it."

My brain fog refused to lift. "Wait. I'm making coffee." I set the phone down long enough to load and start the coffee maker.

"Okay, I'm back. Irma is mistaken. Patsy was in my house, but I didn't catch her. Wallace did."

"Wallace who?"

"Binion. He lives next door."

Clair laughed. "Don't be coy. Irma read the police report to me and it doesn't say a word about any man next door."

What's she talking about?

"There's some mistake."

Clair ignored my protest. "Patsy's arrest brought it all together. The police found some of the stolen items at her house, which proves she's the burglar."

I rested against the counter and inhaled the aroma of brewing coffee. "I figured she was the town thief when I found her in my house, but it's hard to believe she killed her own husband." The sound of the gunshot and shattering glass flashed through my memory.

Maybe not so hard.

"Patsy's gun was the same caliber as the one that killed Earl. They're sure it will be confirmed once it's tested. And would you believe it? She has a boyfriend."

I pulled a mug from the cupboard, glaring at the still dripping coffee maker. "We're still talking about Patsy? I don't think so. If that's true, no one at the Rare Curl knew. Stacy would have told me. She can't keep anything to herself."

"Patsy's supposedly in love with some guy. Irma said she clammed up when they asked his name. By the way, how did you get the gun away from her?"

Coffee finally finished, I poured a cup and took a quick slurp. "Ouch. Crap."

"What?"

"Burned my tongue. Umm, I didn't take the gun from her, that would be Wallace."

Clair's loud, drawn-out sigh erupted from the receiver. "Okay girl. You stick with your story. I'm on my way to work and I'll call you later when I hear from Irma. She said they'd question Patsy again this afternoon. Bye now."

It was useless trying to convince Clair. I put down the phone, pulled out a dining chair, and sat.

Mason appeared at my feet, expecting breakfast. His golden eyes caused me to smile. "How do you think Wallace kept his name off the police report?"

Chapter Thirty-six

The sun shone warm on my face as I stepped out onto the porch to wait for Rarity. She wanted to visit Patsy, and to encourage her, maybe to counsel her. I wasn't as charitable. I needed to hear Patsy explain stealing from me, and how the woman could shoot her husband.

The ceramic pot filled with colorful flowers, from Anita, now graced my front porch. I was among the few fortunate theft victims whose items were returned. The plants were beginning to perk up after I'd soaked the soil with water. I'd think if you wanted to steal flowers, you'd know enough to take care of them, so they don't die. Maybe not. Maybe she would have thrown them away and replaced them, using someone else's treasures to decorate her home.

The sound of male laughter caught my attention. Wallace and Jack Spencer emerged from Wallace's house. With a slap on the back, Wallace bid Agent Spencer goodbye and stepped back inside.

He was halfway to his SUV when Agent Spencer turned his face toward me. He stuck his hands in his pockets and cut across the grass in my direction.

I stiffened at his approach, not thrilled about talking to him after my performance at the salon. "Good morning, Agent Spencer."

He smiled, piercing me with his dark eyes. "Call me Jack. I'm afraid we got off on the wrong track, before. I didn't intend to offend you. I know it was a stressful situation but it's over. The court system will take it from here."

I took a deep breath and tried to relax my shoulders. "You were only doing your job, and I was being protective of Patsy. I'm sorry I overreacted. As it turned out, I couldn't have been more wrong about her."

"Loyalty's an admirable quality." He turned to study the street. I noticed his hair was wet and the breeze brought in the light scent of aftershave. "I'm leaving town—called back to the office in Tampa."

He turned back to me and flashed a lop-sided smile. "My work brings me north from time to time, and I try to visit my old friend, Wallace. So I was wondering if next time I'm in town, would you be interested in dinner?"

That made me step back. I stifled a grin. "Umm. Yes. I would like that."

What? Where did that come from?

His grin came easily. "Great. Well, I have to get on the road, but I'll be in touch. I'll make a point of getting back up here." His gaze held mine for a moment before he pivoted and strode to his vehicle.

I watched him walk away, wondering what I'd done. He wasn't even my type—not anything like Marc. Marc's blond hair and blue eyes, artistic temperament. Agent Spencer's dark hair, smoldering eyes, forceful. Nothing alike. Chances are, I wouldn't hear from him. Still, it felt good to have a handsome man—Clair would describe as delicious—show some interest in me.

The purr of Rarity's VW Bug drew my attention to where she parked, facing the wrong way at the curb. She leaned out the window. "Oh my, look at that broken glass. When will they replace it?"

I trotted to her car and lowered myself into the passenger seat. "Sometime this week. I'll be relieved when it's fixed."

"It's a blessing, that was the only casualty, and thank goodness Wallace was home to help you."

"I'm grateful. By the way, you're the only one who believes me. How did Wallace manage to keep his name off the police report?"

"What do you mean, dear? Would they need his name for boarding your window?"

"No, I mean. . ." I caught the twinkle in her eye, leaned back, and opted to admire the blue sky as we drove.

Rarity turned the volume down on the radio, "It's kind of you to visit Patsy. I hope you can forgive her. She needs to know she has friends, even though she's made mistakes."

"I don't know about that. She killed Earl and shot

at me. I could be dead or in the hospital. She stole Aunt Ruth's antique vases. Thank goodness, she still had them. She even had my first house warming gift from Anita. I had no idea it was missing."

"I understand your feelings. It was terribly wrong, and Patsy must pay for her crimes." Rarity flipped on her turn signal, checked traffic, and merged onto Main Street. "I want her to know God loves her, and there is forgiveness. We all commit crimes, if not against the law of the land, against God. None of us deserves it, but He forgives in spite of us. Of course, I don't condone what she did, but God wants us to have a heart full of love."

I blew out a long breath. "I know you're right. Forgiveness. I don't understand it but I'll work on it." The VW jolted to a stop in the lot adjacent to the historic, stone building that housed the Evelynton jail.

~

Hot, stale air hit my throat in a stranglehold, as we entered the windowless room where we would meet Patsy. Rarity and I sat side by side in metal chairs, waiting.

When she appeared, Patsy seemed more comfortable than I felt. A slight smile tugged at her lips. The guard took his place in the corner, far enough away as not to be obvious while he listened to our conversation.

Rarity smiled sweetly. "How are you? Are they treating you well?"

Patsy rested her hands on the table, almost as if they weren't handcuffed. "I'm glad you came. I think I should tell you I'm leaving the salon. Remember, Rarity, when my sister and her husband promised I could live with them in Florida if anything happened to Earl?"

"Yes, I remember. You told me how much you love palm trees."

Patsy's eyes sparkled. "The weather is beautiful down there. They have flowers blooming all year round, and pick oranges right off a tree in their back yard. Can you imagine?"

Patsy lost her smile and slammed back against her chair. "Course, I knew that was just talk. They wouldn't really want me. Not enough room."

After a moment, she brightened and the smile returned. "But Phillip's going to take me. Do you remember Phillip Townsend? He came in for haircuts. He's a charmer, and so handsome."

Rarity nodded and put her hand on Patsy's. "He made quite an impression with all the girls."

I gasped, wanting to tell Rarity she shouldn't touch the prisoner, but resisted grabbing her hand.

Patsy's yellowed teeth showed as she grinned, "But he only wanted to see me. Treated me as if I was the only woman in the world. He always asked my opinion on things and valued my suggestions." Patsy lifted her chin and cooed her story. "Did you know he came back every two weeks for a cut, and even brought me candy?" If it weren't for the bleak surroundings, Patsy could've been sitting in her kitchen, innocently chatting with friends.

Rarity smiled into her eyes. "Yes Patsy, he did

seem taken with you."

Rarity was behaving as if she was in Patsy's kitchen, too. *Good grief woman, she's a murderer.*

Patsy nodded. "And always the perfect gentleman." A sneer crossed her face. "When Earl worked late—he always worked late—Philip took me out to the diner at the edge of town. You didn't know that, did you?"

"No. That was nice of him."

"Phillip thinks I'm too special to work so hard. He said we'd go to Florida and live in style."

Patsy lifted her shoulders and smiled as if she had a secret she couldn't wait to tell. "That's when we got the idea. While at the salon, I discovered who had valuables we could sell, and Phillip taught me how to break into their houses. Then he took the goods to Warrenton, sold it, and saved the money for us."

"Phillip said Earl didn't appreciate what he had." Color appeared in Patsy's neck and crept into her cheeks. "And then Earl started talking about Helen Peters. Said she was cute. He'd go to the nursing home to see his uncle Ned, and come home with something to say about little blond Helen, and what a good job she did." Patsy panted and spat out words. "He thought she was better than me. Well, I'd had enough of that."

I shifted my gaze to the guard. Far from a reassuring presence, he was talking into his cell phone.

"I came up with the idea to kill Earl and collect the life insurance money so we'd have plenty for Florida. Phillip admired me for thinking of that."

Patsy clamped her mouth shut and fell silent for a full thirty seconds, then threw her head back and produced a laugh that echoed off the bare walls. "You know Helen comes into the salon. She has to have someone young do her hair, so she goes to Stacy. Well, I swept up some of those blond hairs the last time she had a cut, and I put them in a little baggie. Then I picked up her coffee cup, put it in a bag, and took that with me."

Patsy lifted her eyebrows and studied Rarity and me, waiting for her words sink in. And they did. Patsy was more homicidal than I'd imagined.

"Earl had an old gun in the closet—been there for years. He said it belonged to his father. He kept it loaded and ordered me to stay away. As if I wasn't good enough to touch the old man's gun. Well, Earl raved about that hussy Helen one too many times." Patsy's nostrils flared and her eyes widened.

Rarity and I exchanged a glance. In the ten minutes we'd been with Patsy, her expression had flown from sweet smile, to angry, wild-eyed sneer, raving lunatic, and back again.

Patsy leaned in and whispered. "Earl worked late one night, so I took that gun, the coffee cup, and the baggie of hair. Philip drove. He said he would shoot Earl for me, but it would be good for me to do it myself. Closure, you know? He dropped me off and I sneaked in the side door."

She slapped the table prompting us to jerk back in our chairs. "They always hide a key under the mat. Earl didn't even hear me come in."

"He—" Patsy guffawed. "He noticed me standing in his office, and said, real snotty like, 'What the 'h' are you doing here?' I told him, 'I'm going to Florida.' And I shot him." She formed her hand into the shape of a gun and aimed it at me. "Pow!"

Embarrassing as it is to admit, I jumped and almost fell off my chair. Rarity gazed at me with big eyes and pursed lips. We were speechless.

Patsy continued. "Listen to this. Philip was so proud of me for thinking of it. I wore rubber gloves—the ones I use at the shop for hair color. I left the coffee cup on Earl's desk and put a couple of Helen's bleached hairs on his chest."

She appraised us from the corner of her eye and winked. "I figured all that out watching crime shows."

She clasped her cuffed hands and pounded the table. "It would have worked, too, if Helen hadn't been playing Bingo with Melvin's wife. Should've been home where she belonged."

At that point, Patsy gazed intently at the wall behind us.

I leaned forward and softened my voice, wondering how to ask without upsetting her. "You were in my house twice. Why was that?"

Her eyes darted to me. "Three times. Well, I only got as far as the back porch, the first time. The second time, I got some good stuff. But Phillip said I had to go back again and he came with me."

I sat up straight. "Phillip, in my house?" I'd walked in while there were two intruders?

"Oh yeah. He wanted something of yours.

Something in particular. He searched downstairs while I went upstairs." Patsy narrowed her eyes and glared. "You came home."

She returned her attention to the wall and shrugged her shoulders. "He got away. I was too slow." Patsy's features began to sag and then crumpled into a picture of profound sadness.

"What did Phillip want?" I received no response. "Patsy?"

Rarity reached to clasp Patsy's hand but seemed to think better of it. "Is there anything I can bring you, to make you more comfortable?"

Patsy stared at the wall.

Rarity tried again, this time in a whisper, but received no reaction. She turned to me. "I think we'd better go."

"I think you're right." I whispered goodbye to Patsy, and Rarity assured her she would visit again. Patsy gave no indication of having heard.

~

We pushed through the heavy door and stepped into the sunshine. I took a deep cleansing breath. It felt like my first breath since we entered that dismal gray room.

Rarity murmured. "Patsy will be better off if Philip Townsend never comes back."

"I doubt he ever planned to take her with him. I've heard that name before."

Rarity's red curls flew as her head swiveled toward me. "You have?"

"My friend Clair dated him. She said he was very

attentive but then dropped her suddenly. That must have been about the time he found Patsy—someone easier to influence."

"Your friend and then your coworker. And your house. Why did he want in your house? What do you think he was looking for?"

"I don't have a clue, but if he found anything, he can have it. In any event, I've learned to keep my doors locked and my gun handy."

Rarity put her hand to her forehead and squeezed her eyes shut. "Oh dear. Well, they know his identity, and they'll catch him. And Wallace is right next door. I know Wallace will keep an eye on you."

When we reached the car, Rarity leaned on the roof. "Poor Patsy. I should've seen it. I knew she was unhappy but never thought it could go this far. I hadn't realized how much she depended on a man for self-esteem."

"Phillip Townsend found an easy mark."

We climbed into the car and as she fastened her seat belt, Rarity shook her head. "Can't believe I missed the signs. I feel as if I failed her. I'll visit as often as they let me. She needs to know there is forgiveness, no matter what she's done. She needs to understand how special she is in God's eyes."

Rarity shifted the car into gear and steered it into traffic.

I gazed out the window, watching the trees go by, and considered the possibility of a true crime novel based on the crimes of this very disturbed woman. Would I be able to understand Patsy's reasoning?

When had her mental illness begun? Something in her childhood? Was it the mental or verbal abuse of her husband? How did everyone, especially those of us who worked with her, miss her desperate need for recognition? Was everyone, like me, too concerned with their own problems? Yet, Philip Townsend so easily identified her as his target.

No. I couldn't write about Patsy. I couldn't profit from her sadness. If anything, I'll go along with Rarity to encourage her.

Chapter Thirty-seven

Rarity pulled her VW to the curb in front of my house. Her eyes rimmed in red, I'd never seen her so weary. "I'll see you at work next week. I'll be so relieved when everything is back to normal at the salon."

I climbed out of the car and leaned down to speak through the window. "Me too. It would great if life could be routine for a change."

I took my time walking across the yard. How long had it been since I appreciated the cool shade of the maple tree? The bird songs seemed particularly melodious and sweet.

As I climbed the steps, my cell rang and I fished it out of my bag.

"Hi girlfriend, it's Clair."

"Nice to hear your cheerful voice. It's been a long day. Rarity and I. . . "

"Guess what, I just got a new listing."

I should have known I wouldn't get through a

complete thought.

"Paul Cooper's house. He and Missy are moving to her hometown in Iowa. They made a snap decision over the weekend and have already called a moving company." Clair erupted in giggles. "Guess you'll never solve the case of the impostor classmate."

"Stop. You won't let me live that one down, will you?" The truth bubbled up inside my brain but I reminded myself it would help no one. "I'm sure Missy will enjoy being back in her hometown."

"I was surprised Paul didn't want to sell the house himself, or at least list with Perry, but. . . . Hold on, someone's at the door."

A moment later, Clair whispered through the phone. "Whoa. This is my lucky day. It's Mr. Beautiful himself, Agent Spencer. Talk to you later, bye."

A beep signaled the broken connection, so I put my phone back in my bag and proceeded inside. Agent Spencer? I thought he left town this morning.

The cat waited for me in the kitchen. "Mason, time to get into an orderly existence. I'm going to sweep up the cat food you left scattered around your dish, and wash the kitchen floor. You go chase butterflies, and later we'll watch a movie."

~

Mason and I settled on the sofa. I cradled a bowl of popcorn and flipped channels in search of an afternoon flick. Rapping on the door infringed on the tranquility.

"Oh please. I'd hoped for a quiet, peaceful afternoon." I set aside the bowl and plodded to the door.

Clair stood on the porch with her hands on her hips and cheeks pinker than I'd ever seen them.

She strode in as soon as the door swung open and proceeded to pace around the living room, hands in constant motion. "Girl, you won't believe it. I sure can't."

Mason trotted behind her and made two circuits before he leapt to the coffee table, to track her with his eyes.

The story of Philip Townsend came in bits and pieces. I'd retreated to the sofa, and remained mute while Clair circled the room spending pent-up anger and spouting her hurt and frustration.

"I can't believe I fell for Philip's line. Jack, that's Agent Spencer, trailed him to Evelynton. Said something about Philip being a witness in a murder case in Florida. It's weird because that crime was committed five years ago."

"A murder? Did Agent Spencer say where in Florida?"

"Umm. Tampa, I think. Isn't that where you lived?"

Clair's voice rose a few decibels. "And, listen to this. Philip had even served four years in prison, for larceny. Who would have thought, me with an ex-con? When he got out, Philip told the police he'd heard a cellmate admit to a shooting. He'd testify, but he wanted witness protection. But then the fool got scared and left the state."

Clair groaned and continued. "What a loser. Jack called him a sociopath and said he's adept at taking advantage of women. I guess I have first-hand knowledge of that."

Clair stopped and put her fists on her hips. "Would you believe I blamed myself when he dropped me? Thought it was something I'd done, or I was working too many hours, when in reality, he'd found an easier mark—Patsy Clooney. She became his partner and gathered all kinds of information for his criminal pursuits." Clair glanced at the boarded window. "Too bad you were one of the victims."

My throat closed around the questions popping into my head.

Clair stomped to the door and clutched the knob. "Jack said he was sure the jerk wouldn't be back this way. His contacts say Philip's been seen driving back south. Mark my words, this is the last time you'll ever hear me speak the name, Philip Townsend. I'm better than that and I'm moving on."

Clair paused and an innocent smile transformed her face. "I'm hoping Agent Spencer will be back. I think he has ties to someone here in town."

"Right now, I'm off to sell a house." She opened the door and made her exit, shutting it firmly behind her.

Hitchcock's <u>Rear Window</u> played on the TV, but I pulled Mason into my lap and turned my attention to the door of the now empty closet beneath the staircase.

Chapter Thirty-eight

I opened my eyes to the last beams of afternoon sunlight filtering through the dining room windows. The boarded window in the living room dimmed the light enough to accommodate peaceful napping, my new pastime. I'd always referred to the need for naps as a small town habit. Now it was mine, not intentional, but comforting. I was beginning to see the benefits. Mason appreciated a good nap, too, seldom letting me sleep alone.

His body was draped over my stomach. Nudging him as gently as possible, I lifted him to the floor and wondered what was in the kitchen for supper.

The sound of crunching gravel in my driveway, and a slamming car door alerted me to the approaching visitor. The thud of leather soles on the porch and the knock brought me to my feet.

The narrow window in the door revealed Jack Spencer leaning against the railing, eyes focused down the street. I took a moment to admire his strong arms folded across his chest, then ran my fingers through my hair and attempted to smooth wrinkles from my shirt, before pulling the door open.

"Hello, Agent Spencer. This is a surprise. I thought you would've been out of the state by this time."

Deep brown eyes ignited a fluttering in my stomach. His smile was warm but held a strange tentative glimmer. I doubted this was a social call.

"Um. Please come in."

"I'd planned to be out of here, but got a phone call, from the jail, before I reached the city limits. It kept me in town a bit longer than expected." Jack took a seat on the sofa, rested his elbows on his knees, and waited for me to sit.

The fluttering in my stomach turned to queasiness. Could this drama please be over?

I sat in the side chair, mute, waiting for the show to begin again.

He cleared his throat and began to recant the story Clair related earlier.

"Agent Spencer, allow me to interrupt, to save time. Clair Lane came over after you talked to her, and told me about Philip Townsend."

"Good, that does save time. But I'm afraid she didn't have the whole story. I questioned Ms. Lane about Townsend and related everything that pertained to her situation. Townsend has fled the state. My sources tell me he's probably in Georgia at the moment."

Jack continued. "Ms. Halloren, I understand your late husband was a professional photographer?"

Marc?

"Photo Journalist." I nodded and waited for the bomb to drop.

"How much do you know about your husband's pursuits?"

"I don't know what you mean by pursuits, but I know everything about him. He had a great job. Travel, excitement. His assignments took him out of the country a lot. I went with him most of the time. We traveled to some exotic places, beautiful mountains, sunny beaches. Some of his assignments were dangerous—war zones or dictatorships. Then, of course, I'd stay home."

"Did he show you his work—his photographs?"

"Sure. Well, not always. He'd mainly share the great scenery, landscapes, some of famous people. He was protective, didn't want to expose me to the atrocities. Sometimes I'd wait for the magazine to come out and sneak out to buy it. Other times, he wouldn't even tell me what magazine he'd worked for."

Agent Spencer's eyes grew intense. He gazed at me while I spoke, seeming to sift through and weigh my words.

I took a deep breath and blew it out. "What is this about? What has my husband to do with you?"

"Let's go back to the beginning. Ms. Lane told you about Philip Townsend. He'd been in witness protection. I had charge of him until he could testify. We think the local drug lord found him, and he made a deal. He ran and I lost track of him until he turned up here in Evelynton."

"You lost him? Must have been embarrassing for you, but what's the point of all this?" I wished I would have worded that a little nicer. But it had been a long day and I wanted it to be over.

A half-smile lifted his face. "Yes. It was embarrassing, to say the least. The point is we think Townsend followed you here in hopes of finding some incriminating photos your husband may have had in his possession. They would have been of drug activity. If that's the case, we need to take possession of them, and know why Halloren didn't report what he saw."

"Excuse me?"

"The crime Townsend offered information on was a drug-related murder. Marc Halloren's shooting death."

The bomb, I knew was coming, exploded and I saw stars.

"Halloren witnessed and photographed the transfer of drugs, off the coast of Florida. Again, we wonder why it wasn't reported."

"No, you've got the wrong man. Marc died in a drive-by shooting. Random, like a gang initiation." I enunciated each word carefully, willing them to be heard and understood. "That's what the police said and the investigation proved. The case is closed."

Jack remained calm. His voice soothing, as he gazed into my eyes. "I understand that's what you were told, from the information they had at that time, their best guess. The case was never closed. But with the information Townsend gave us—"

I clenched my hands in my lap and noticed they were wet. Hadn't even realized tears streamed down my face.

I struggled to get words out. There was barely enough breath in my lungs to make myself heard. "No, that's wrong. It was random. Marc was simply in the wrong place at the wrong time. This can't be true." I wrapped my arms around myself to still the shaking.

Jack stood and pulled me out of the chair, and into his arms. I leaned into his chest and let my tears seep into his shirt.

"I'm sorry, Lauren. Probably a misunderstanding. Maybe he photographed something else, and never saw the transfer taking place in the background."

I nodded, my face still buried in his shirt. That was it. All a misunderstanding.

"What we do need is any files of his or photographs you may have."

I pushed away and ran my hands over my face. "I don't have any of Marc's files. That Townsend guy may have found something. The boxes had been ripped open. It was all a mess that night, and Wallace offered to take it to the trash. I told him to go ahead. I wanted it out of my house."

"To the trash? Wallace threw them out? When was this? Where did he take them?" Jack still held my shoulders. His eyes had widened and locked into mine.

Pulling my eyes away, I jerked free of his grasp and backed up, putting a chair between us. "Right after the break-in, the night they caught Patsy Clooney. Everything's gone. The garbage truck has come since

216

then."

"So you're saying any evidence there might have been, is gone? All the files? You must have something. What else do you have belonging to your husband?"

I squeezed my hands into fists, and shrieked, "Yes, all his files are gone, ask Wallace. Wait, I have Marc's favorite mug. I suppose that's evidence. Do you want to take his coffee cup? It's cleverly hidden on the windowsill in the kitchen." I regretted the outburst and misplaced sense of humor, as soon as it left my big mouth.

Jack raised his hands in surrender. Beads of perspiration had formed on his forehead. "Well, no. Sorry Lauren. Not your fault. I'm confident you didn't purposely dispose of evidence."

"Of course, I didn't purposely dispose of evidence. This is crazy. There wasn't any evidence. Marc had nothing to do with drugs."

Agent Spencer acted as if he hadn't heard.

"Chances are Townsend found what he was looking for and is delivering it back to his contact in Florida, or he's destroyed it. I'll be on his trail as soon as I leave here."

Sorry didn't get it. I felt flames licking the inside of my chest, and the blaze was building. I stretched myself up to my full height, lifted my chin to glare into his brown eyes, and raised my sweaty fists in defiance. "My husband was an honest man and had nothing to do with any drug transfer. This is all a lie."

Agent Spencer backed toward the door, his hands still raised—maybe in defense. "Calm down. I'm sure you're right. I'll catch up with Townsend. And when I do, this will all be cleared up. I promise."

He side-stepped off the porch, eyes darting between me and the steps. Once he'd retreated to the SUV, he turned to face me. Lines etched his forehead. "Look, I'm sorry. Don't worry about it. We'll discover the truth, and I'll contact you." He paused. "Lauren, I'll see you again."

I grabbed the doorknob and flung the door closed with all my strength. The sound of slamming echoed like a gunshot.

~

The cat food box slipped from my hand and kibble spilled onto the counter when I heard the news anchor. He seemed to be shouting. The old T.V. did that sometimes. The volume would increase for no reason. Other times I could hardly hear it.

This morning the words rushed in to the kitchen from the living room, loud and clear. He said Fort De Soto Park on St. Joan Key. It was the name that caught my attention. Marc and I had spent many happy hours walking that beach. Miles of white sand, blue skies and clear water.

I walked to the living room to watch. The newsman reported of the body of a man found washed up on the beach. This wasn't an overly odd occurrence for the national news. No reason to concern me. I wouldn't have listened if it hadn't been on that beach.

The badly decomposed body was thought to have been in the warm water of Tampa bay for several days, possibly longer. Police determined the deceased to be

Philip Townsend. The manner of death was not immediately apparent. But, hopefully, this would be determined by the autopsy.

I was still processing this news later in the afternoon, and answered the phone without checking for caller ID.

The warm, manly voice stunned me. "Lauren, it's Jack Spencer. I assume you heard the news report this morning. Philip Townsend's dead."

"I heard." I held my breath, despite his friendly, almost intimate tone. What bombshell did Agent Spencer have in his arsenal, today?

"We don't know yet how he died. He didn't have anything on him except his driver's license and a motel room key. We searched the room and turned up nothing."

I took a deep breath. "So, what does that mean?"

"It means you don't have to worry about Townsend. He won't be back, and unless the autopsy turns up something interesting, I'm recommending we close the case."

"I see." The news slowly entered my brain.

"My report is that Townsend came back empty handed from Evelynton, and is now deceased. We'll find out later this week, how he died. He was a small-time hood and a liar. My guess is he lied to one person too many. We have only his word there were ever any photos. Most likely, he fabricated the whole story, and got caught up in it when some thug came after him."

I didn't care what happened to Townsend. "Marc's name is cleared?"

"As far as I'm concerned, there is no reason to suspect your late husband of any wrongdoing. I think they were correct in the random shooting verdict, and I'm closing the case."

"Okay. Thanks for letting me know." My voice came out in a whisper as the strength left my body. My knees weakened. "Umm. I have to go."

"Sure. I just wanted you to know. Maybe I'll talk to you later. Take care."

The line went dead, along with that part of my life.

Chapter Thirty-nine

Wicker chairs on the back porch. Three women cradled hot coffee against the cool morning breeze. A cat purred in his sleep. Just a few benefits of the small town life I'd begun to love.

Anita leaned back and propped her feet up on the old wicker table. "Has Rarity hired a new hairdresser yet?"

"Not yet. She and Stacey have been working extra hours to get everyone in. Patsy's customers still want to rehash the whole story, and Rarity has had to spend extra time with each one. They all need reassurance that Patsy really did go off the deep end and kill Earl. She admitted it to us."

"Now that the chaos has settled, things are returning to normal. I expect Rarity will place a help wanted ad soon."

Clair set her cup down and inspected her manicure. "How's the writing coming? Very far along on that novel?"

"No."

That answer was too abrupt. I've promised myself not to make up stories in the future. But how long will it take to get out of this one?

"Umm. I put it aside. Taking time to breathe after all the real-life drama in this town. I'm catching up on magazine articles and working on a piece for the newspaper. It's about the Beaver Creek residents."

"The nursing home? That's something new for you, isn't it?"

"It's a first for me. I sort of fell into it by mistake, but the old people are fun to talk to. You wouldn't believe the memories and wisdom housed in that nursing home."

Anita placed her mug on the table and stretched her arms above her head. "It's going to be a beautiful day. Let's go for a picnic later. We'll go to Firemen's Park. They have some nice picnic tables and we can watch the children play on the playground equipment. Do you have any appointments, Clair?"

"I was going to work in the office today. My first appointment is tomorrow morning—the Cooper closing. That house was the smoothest transaction I've ever experienced. Everybody, who looked at it, wanted it. Paul and Missy must have been the cleanest couple ever. Every inch spotless, and not a loose screw or crooked blind in the whole place. Couldn't even tell there'd been a car in the garage. It's as if they were storybook people. I think they led a charmed life."

"Things aren't always as they seem. Sometimes

perfect people are just well versed at hiding their secrets." I took a swig of coffee to shut myself up.

Clair grinned. "Not every book is a mystery, Lauren. Sometimes it's a love story. And those two were as close to a leading couple as you can get."

And sometimes it's both a mystery and a love story.

Clair sighed and directed her attention to Anita. "A picnic is a wonderful idea. I'll take the day off."

Two women's faces swiveled in my direction. Even Mason lifted his head to look at me.

"I can take today off, too. I'll make sandwiches. Who's bringing the salad?"

The End

74669159R00138

Made in the USA
Columbia, SC
03 August 2017